danny constantino's FIRST (AND MAYBE LAST?) DATE

PAUL ACAMPORA

Dial Books for Young Readers

Dial Books for Young Readers
An imprint of Penguin Random House LLC, New York

First published in the United States of America by Dial Books for Young Readers,
an imprint of Penguin Random House LLC, 2020

Visit us online at penguinrandomhouse.com.

Library of Congress Cataloging-in-Publication Data
Names: Acampora, Paul, author. Title: Danny Constantino's first (and maybe last?) date / Paul
Acampora. Description: New York : Dial Books for Young Readers, [2020] | Audience: Ages 9–12.
| Audience: Grades 4–6. | Summary: Between going to the middle school dance with his celebrity
crush and watching his mom campaign to be the next town mayor, Danny has a lot to learn
about life in the spotlight.
Identifiers: LCCN 2019054656 (print) | LCCN 2019054657 (ebook) | ISBN 9781984816610
(hardcover) | ISBN 9781984816627 (ebook)
Subjects: CYAC: Dating (Social customs)—Fiction. | Celebrities—Fiction. | Elections—Fiction. |
Middle schools—Fiction. | Schools—Fiction.
Classification: LCC PZ7.A17298 Dan 2020 (print) | LCC PZ7.A17298 (ebook) | DDC [Fic]—dc23

10 9 8 7 6 5 4 3 2 1

Design by Cerise Steel
Text set in Aldus LT

For Debbie, Nicholas & Gabrielle

Table of Contents

Chapter 1

tripping over ghosts

I do not believe in ghosts, but that doesn't stop me from tripping over the spirit of my dead dog and falling flat on my face to start the day.

Jacko, a big mutt who was basically a cross between a Labrador retriever and an orange bulldozer, always claimed the same spot at the bottom of our stairs. Like Jacko, I am a creature of habit. Unfortunately, my dog has been gone since summer. It's October now, and I'm racing around to get ready for school. I sprint down the steps and jump over the place where Jacko—short for Jack-o'-lantern—used to sleep. Mid-leap, I remember that Jacko's not here anymore.

It is fair to say that I do not stick the landing.

Instead, I trip, tuck, roll, and smash into our front door, which is located a few feet away from the bottom of the stairs.

Mom steps out of the upstairs bathroom and leans

over the railing. She's got a curling iron in one hand and a hairbrush in the other. She's wearing a dark blue skirt and super high heels, which means she's getting ready to show a very expensive house this morning. According to my mother—the number one real estate agent in all of Cuper Cove, Massachusetts, if you believe her business cards—the higher the price, the higher the heels.

"Danny," she calls down to me, "did you knock over my campaign stuff?"

Our stairs are covered with pamphlets, posters, and lawn signs because Mom wants to be Cuper Cove's next mayor, and the election is just a few weeks away.

"I tripped over Jacko," I explain.

"Danny," Mom says. "Jacko is dead."

As if I didn't know. Of course, the fact that I'm sprawled on the floor does make it look like I might need a reminder.

"Sometimes it feels like he's still here."

"Earth to Danny," says Mom while she runs the brush through her hair. "Yesterday is gone. Focus on today."

I turn my head toward the collection of photos sitting inside a display cabinet near the front door. Every frame holds a picture of my father, a man I don't remember because he died when I was still in diapers.

Mom sees what I'm looking at. "Your father is a different story," she says, and returns to the bathroom.

She's right. Jacko was around lots longer than my

dad. Also, Jacko died at home. My father, Marine 1st Lieutenant Matthew Owens, died on duty. He's a big hero in our town, and Mom likes to tell everybody that I'll be going to the United States Naval Academy one day too. It's a prediction that always gets a round of applause on her campaign trail, but I'm not so sure about the marines in my future.

While I definitely appreciate my father's service, and I'm very glad he was around long enough to help bring me into this world, I don't know that I want to follow in his footsteps. First of all, my only battle-ready role models are make-believe superheroes and comic book characters. That's probably not enough to get me ready for real-life military service. I'm not even sure if it's enough to get me through middle school. Second, my Dad's footsteps would be lots more interesting if he wasn't dead.

Before I can get to my feet, our front door swings open. My grandmother, who lives just a few blocks away, steps inside. Gram is gray-haired, blue-eyed, short, and petite. Unlike Mom, who is a blond, high-heeled, dressed-for-success kind of person, my grandmother wears jeans, comfy shoes, and a loose sweater every day. She's the school secretary at Cuper Cove Middle School, where I've been a seventh grader for about eight weeks. Gram's been there since the beginning of time. These days she's like the unofficial school mascot. Our official mascot is a unicorn named Cooper.

Gram takes a look at me on the floor. "Did you trip over Jacko, again?"

I sit up. "I keep forgetting he's gone."

"I still put a plate out for your grandfather sometimes, and he's been gone for thirty years." She offers a hand and helps me to my feet. "I'm parked at the curb. Are you riding with me today?"

Mom reappears at the top of the stairs. "Danny's taking the bus to school," she announces.

I don't mind the school bus, but given a choice I'd rather ride in Gram's car. It's an old green Camaro with awesome black racing stripes, front and rear spoilers, shiny chrome wheels, and dual exhaust pipes that roar like a squadron of fighter jets when Gram punches the gas. Seriously, who wouldn't choose the Camaro? Unfortunately, I do not seem to have a choice today.

Mom trots down the stairs and squeezes past Gram and me. "I want you to give something to Shad," she tells me.

"Who's Shad?" I ask.

"Your bus driver," says Gram.

"Mr. Beamon?"

"The one and only," Mom calls back.

Mr. Beamon is a tall, skinny white guy with a short beard and a long black ponytail. He wears a red flannel jacket, and he decorates the school bus dashboard with toy spaceships and pine tree fresheners so the bus always smells like Christmas. He also keeps a stack of fat books beside his seat, and he gives out tiny toy gumball machine monsters if he thinks you need one. On the day Mom announced her campaign for mayor, Mr. Beamon offered me a small plastic bunny rabbit wielding a carrot like an orange broadsword.

"What's this for?" I asked him.

"Some people carry a rabbit's foot for luck." Mr. Beamon nodded toward Mom's face on a MISSY FOR MAYOR sign already planted on a lawn across the street from school. "Living with the mayor will require the whole rabbit."

"She's not the mayor yet," I said.

"Do you think she knows that?" Mr. Beamon asked.

I accepted the battle bunny.

Now Gram and I follow Mom into the kitchen, where she reaches into a cabinet and pulls out a fat white mug. On one side of the cup, small, neat letters say YOUR FAVORITE REALTOR, MISSY CONSTANTINO! On the other side, bold, black script promises that EVERYTHING I TOUCH TURNS TO SOLD! She hands me the cup.

"For me?" I say.

"For Shad. I hear he's putting his house up for sale." Mom tucks one of her business cards into the mug. "And give him my best."

"What kind of name is Shad?"

"Ask him yourself," says Mom.

"Shad is a kind of fish," Gram tells me.

Mom glances at her wristwatch. It's one of those high-tech things that checks your pulse, takes your phone calls, orders your groceries, and sings you to sleep. Believe it or not, it tells time too. "I'm running behind," Mom says, then mutters a quick prayer. "Saint Expeditus, speed my way."

"Saint Expeditus?" I ask.

"Patron saint against being late." Mom's got a saint and a prayer for everything.

"Once upon a time," Gram says, "your mother didn't even want to get married in a church. Now she turns the saints into her own personal assistants."

"Danny knows that his father and I never married." Mom grabs a stack of papers off the kitchen table and shoves them into a fat black briefcase. "I'd change that if I could, but I can't."

I rub my knee. "What's the saint for falling down the stairs?"

"Saint Stanislaus Kostka is patron saint of broken bones." Mom zips her briefcase shut and then plants a quick kiss on my forehead. "But let's not give Saint Stan any work today."

A moment later, the door slams shut behind her.

Gram turns to me. "Your mother and I don't see eye

to eye on everything, but I agree with her when it comes to Stan. Please try to avoid activities that lead to broken bones, okay?"

"How's that going to work in the marines?" I ask.

"You're not joining the marines, Danny."

An argument about whether or not a seventh grader should join the marines might seem silly except that it's caused temper tantrums, name calling, and ruined dinners between my mother and grandmother for over a decade now. Meanwhile, I can barely walk downtown anymore without somebody complimenting me on my patriotism or thanking me for my future service.

Did I mention that I'm in seventh grade?

"Did you really trip over Jacko?" Gram asks me.

I cross the kitchen, open the refrigerator, and grab the brown-bag lunch I put together last night. "It sure felt that way."

Gram leans forward and puts a hand under my chin. At school she handles bites, bruises, cuts, scrapes, loose teeth, and other assorted minor medical emergencies. Now she stares into my eyes while she tips my head up, down, back and forth. "Are you feeling okay?"

"I think so."

"And Jacko?"

"I still miss him."

Gram glances down at my feet. "But isn't it nice to have shoes without holes chewed in them?"

"That bothered Mom more than it bothered me," I tell her. "And best friends are worth having cold feet."

Gram releases my face, which I guess means no concussion, cracked skull, or brain contusions. "Love is not a church raffle," she says. "You don't always have to be present to win."

"What are you talking about?" I ask.

"Just because Jacko's gone doesn't mean he's not here anymore."

"That doesn't make any sense."

Gram laughs. "I tell your grandfather the same thing every day."

Chapter 2

bring on the dancing tigers

On days that I take the bus, I meet up with my best friend, Ajay Kalli, who lives less than four minutes away if I jog through three backyards, hop over one wooden fence, and avoid Marcel, an unchained black-and-white Russell terrier who doesn't bite but won't let me pass unless I toss him a tennis ball at least a couple dozen times.

Ten minutes later, because Marcel spotted me, I'm seated at Ajay's dining room table, where he's filling up on dosas and fruit chutney.

"Good morning, Danny." Mrs. Kalli, wearing a loose, flowery housedress, steps out of the kitchen and puts a plate in front of me.

I already ate a piece of cold pizza at home, but I don't push the food away because first of all, I love dosas and chutney. Second of all, trying to say no to Ajay's mom is pointless. "Thanks, Mrs. Kalli."

"You're a good boy," she tells me. "You know what a good breakfast is supposed to look like."

I don't mention the pizza.

Mrs. Kalli points at Ajay's big sister, Asha, who is scooping up neon-colored cereal from a bowl filled with lime-green milk. "This one eats candy for breakfast."

"It is not candy." Asha, a junior at Cuper Cove High School, points at the cereal box. "It's made with all-natural whole-grain ingredients fortified with vitamins and minerals to start your day right."

Neither Ajay nor I have any real medical knowledge, but even we know where lime-green milk and marsh-mallow cereal should live on the food pyramid.

"It's still candy," I tell Asha.

Ajay nods. "Definitely candy."

Asha grins, pushes long black hair out of the way, and drinks the last of the green milk straight out of the bowl. "Maybe that's why it's magically delicious." She wipes her face with a sleeve. "And speaking of magical, have you two come up with ideas for this year's Halloween costumes?"

Some people might say seventh graders are too old for Halloween costumes, but that's not true in our town. Cuper Cove's annual Halloween festival, which is less than three weeks away, is the biggest event of the year. Everybody's part of it, including Asha, because, in addition to being tall and smart and pretty, she is a total theater geek. At Cuper Cove High School, she makes costumes and works on stage crew for the plays and musicals. Asha's constructed wings for Tinker Bell, sewed ball gowns for Cinderella, and built a giant singing dragon puppet for Shrek. With Asha's help, Ajay and I have dressed for Halloween as giant robots, X-wing fighter pilots, the Batmobile, several different superheroes, and a cow.

Not two cows. Just one cow.

It seemed like a good idea at the time.

"You could be Pulikali dancers," Mrs. Kalli suggests.

I look up from my dosas. "What are Pulikali dancers?"

Ajay rolls his eyes. "Here we go."

"When I was a little girl in India," Mrs. Kalli tells me, "my parents would take me to the Swaraj Round to see Pulikali during the Hindu Onam festivities. It was very exciting."

I have no idea what Mrs. Kalli is talking about.

"You left out the tigers," Asha tells her mom.

I glance between Asha and Mrs. Kalli. "Tigers?"

Mrs. Kalli laughs. "That is the point, Danny. *Puli* means 'tiger,' and *kali* means 'play.'"

"Tiger play?"

"Exactly! During Onam in Kerala, many hundreds of men will spend all day and all night decorating themselves with paints to resemble tigers. Following preparations, they will pounce and leap and dance through the streets for hours and hours in a public display of manly spirit and macho energy. It is quite spectacular."

Asha shakes her head. "I don't think Cuper Cove is ready for a public display of Danny and Ajay's macho spirit."

"Danny is going to be a marine like his father." Apparently, Mrs. Kalli has been at my mother's campaign events. "That is very manly," she adds.

"There are girl marines," Asha tells her mother.

Asha might be the kindest, gentlest, and most creative girl in Cuper Cove, but there is no doubt in my mind that she would be a much better marine than me.

"We've already been a cow," Ajay reminds everybody. "How much more manly can you get?"

Mrs. Kalli laughs. "You were a very good cow."

I have no idea whether or not we were a very good cow. The view from my part of the costume was limited. And that's all I'm going to say about that.

I spread chutney on another dosa. "I wouldn't mind going as a dancing tiger."

"You could be Cuper Cove's first Pulikali dancers," says Mrs. Kalli.

"I've got a better idea," says Ajay.

I bite into a chutney-covered dosa and talk with my mouth full. "What could be better than dancing tigers?"

"A Trojan unicorn," says Ajay.

I shake my head. "That's not a real thing."

"And dancing tigers are?"

Good point.

"We can build an actual-size Trojan horse out of cardboard," Ajay tells me. "Then we'll add a horn to turn him into a unicorn."

"You can name him Cooper," says Asha. "You'll be your own school's mascot."

Ajay grins. "Exactly!"

"The actual Trojan horse carried about forty soldiers," I point out.

I know my Greek mythology. I've got the comic book.

"Maybe not *actual* actual size, then," says Ajay. "But still really big."

"As long as it isn't a cow," I say. "I don't want to be another cow."

Asha stands to clear her dishes from the table. "You just don't want to be another cow's rear end."

"Isn't that what I just said?"

"Will you help?" Ajay asks his sister.

"Let me get this straight," says Asha. "You want to build a giant, cardboard, fantasy creature loosely based on Greek mythology?"

Ajay nods. "That's right."

"Do you really think you'll be able to keep me away from that?"

Basically, Ajay has the best big sister in the world.

"But first," Mrs. Kalli announces, "Ajay and Danny have to go to school."

"What about you?" I ask Asha, who, I just noticed, is wearing a pair of plaid pajama bottoms and a sweatshirt that says FREAKY FRIDAY: THE MUSICAL.

"High school is closed today and tomorrow," Asha informs me. "Our teachers have some kind of in-service, so I get a two-day vacation."

"I hope your vacation plans include homework, groceries, and housecleaning," Mrs. Kalli tells Asha. "And in case you're wondering, they do."

Ajay gives his sister a big grin. "Enjoy your vacation."

Asha rolls her eyes, grabs her cereal box off the table, and then heads for the kitchen. She stops before leaving the dining room. "Hey," she says. "Check this out." She reads aloud from the back of the box. *"Every time you buy these hearty and delicious flakes and grains, we donate to the Natalie Flores Griffin Foundation, making your breakfast even sweeter!"* Asha turns to Ajay and me. "Do either of you ever hear from Natalie Flores Griffin?"

Believe it or not, Natalie Flores Griffin—actress, singer, model, and apparently the founder of the Natalie Flores Griffin Foundation—is from Cuper Cove. As a matter of fact, Natalie and I were best friends from kindergarten through fourth grade. But the summer before fifth grade, she and her parents visited a large California amusement park where a tall, talking rodent invited Natalie to step on stage and sing a song. There was a Hollywood agent in the crowd. The rest is history.

"She and I used to email each other for a while," I say. "But then she stopped answering back."

"I heard that her parents divorced." In addition to being a theater geek, Asha's obsessed with Hollywood news, celebrity gossip, and the movies in general.

I shrug. "I think she just got really busy."

"And really famous," says Ajay, who knows I've had a crush on Natalie since forever.

"Maybe that too," I admit.

"But now," says Ajay, "Danny has to settle for being president of the Natalie Flores Griffin Fan Club."

"There's a fan club?" says Asha.

"There is no fan club," I tell her.

Ajay stands and squeezes past Asha to bring his dishes to the sink. "Danny has seen every movie Natalie Flores Griffin ever made," he tells his sister. "I think that counts as a fan club."

"Why don't you call her?" Asha asks me.

"Because she's Natalie Flores Griffin," Ajay calls from the kitchen.

"Wasn't she always Natalie Flores Griffin?" Asha says matter-of-factly.

"Yes," says Ajay, "but now she's NATALIE FLORES GRIFFIN!"

"Well," says Asha, "that clears things up."

I help carry the remaining plates from the dining room to the sink, where Mrs. Kalli offers me a smile. "Natalie might be glad to hear from you, Danny."

"I don't know," I say reluctantly.

"Maybe she and her family would like to visit for the Halloween festival."

"Mom," says Ajay, "this isn't the Pulikali party in Kerala."

"It's true," Mrs. Kalli says a little sadly. "They really know how to throw a party in Kerala."

Asha shoots me a grin. "Maybe Natalie would like to go with you to the Cuper Cove Middle School Halloween festival dance."

Ajay grabs a towel and starts to dry. "That's not going to happen."

"It could be like a date," says Asha.

"It would not be like a date," I tell her.

"As if you wouldn't love to go on a date with Natalie Flores Griffin," Ajay says to me.

"Is that true?" asks Asha.

"Going on a date with Natalie Flores Griffin would not be the worst thing that ever happened to me," I admit.

"So what are you waiting for?" she asks.

Ajay tosses a dish towel at his sister. "How exactly is Danny supposed to ask Natalie Flores Griffin out on a date?"

Asha catches the towel in midair, turns quickly, and whips it at me. "There's this new invention," she says. "It's called the telephone."

I duck but not before the towel smacks me in the face. "I don't have Natalie's phone number."

"Then send her an email," Asha says.

"She probably has a new address by now."

"Or she's got the same email address," says Asha, "and she wonders why the boy she used to know back in Cuper Cove stopped being her friend."

"I didn't stop being her friend."

"You probably wouldn't be a very good date either," Asha adds.

Mrs. Kalli snatches the dish towel away from me before I can throw it at Asha. "Danny would be a very good date," she says.

Asha puts her hands on her hips. "Prove it."

"What exactly do you want me to do?" I pull out my phone and pretend to type a quick message. "Hi, Natalie! Sorry we haven't talked since fourth grade. Want to be my date for the Cuper Cove Halloween festival dance? Trick-or-treat from—"

Before I can finish my sentence, Asha grabs the phone from my hand and races away.

"Hey!" I shout.

Asha swipes at my screen while she runs back into the dining room. "Hi, Natalie!" she says. "Trick-or-treat!"

"Give that back!" I holler.

Asha laughs. "Want to be my date for the Cuper Cove Halloween festival dance? Hope all's well!"

"Asha," Mrs. Kalli says sharply. "Give Danny his phone."

Asha stops with the table between us. She continues to type. "Happy Halloween from your old friend Danny Constantino!"

"Don't worry," Ajay calls from the kitchen. "She doesn't have Natalie's email."

Asha looks up from the phone and grins. "I see Natalie at Natalie the Griffin dot com in your address book. Is that—"

"Yes!" I say. "I mean, no! Don't!"

Asha laughs. "Relax," she tells me. "I didn't hit send."

I sigh. "Thank you."

Asha pokes at my screen. "Now I hit send."

My mouth drops open.

"Danny," says Asha, "what's the worst thing that can happen?"

Before I can reply, the low rumble of a diesel engine thrums in the distance. Ajay, backpack already over his shoulders, steps into the dining room. "That's our bus," he says to me. "We've got to go."

"But—"

He cuts me off. "Relax," he says. "None of this matters.

Movie stars do not go to Halloween dances with seventh graders."

"Natalie's a seventh grader too," Asha reminds her brother.

"She lives in California." Ajay starts toward the door. "She's not coming to Cuper Cove."

"Natalie Flores Griffin can probably fly all over the world anytime she wants," Asha tells him. "Plus, I bet she still has family nearby."

"She would be a very lucky girl to go to the dance with Danny Constantino," Mrs. Kalli offers from the kitchen doorway.

Asha grins. "We'll see about that."

"No," says Ajay. "We won't."

"Danny," says Asha as her brother drags me toward the door, "you were willing to be a dancing tiger. Don't you think a date with Natalie Flores Griffin would be a better way to spend Halloween?"

Dancing tigers versus middle school dance?

Bring on the dancing tigers.

Chapter 3

rom-com for short

"Your sister still has my phone," I tell Ajay once we take our seats on the school bus.

"She'll give it back later," he promises.

"I wish she hadn't done that."

He shrugs. "Welcome to my world."

I stare out the window while Mr. Beamon, who's wearing a gray-and-white ski hat patterned to look like a Death Star from Star Wars, drops the bus into gear. "Hold on tight!" he yells. "Without precise calculations we could fly right through a star or bounce too close to a supernova and that'd end our trip real quick."

"We'll be safe enough once we make the jump to hyperspace," Ajay tells me as we pull away from the curb.

"If that were true," I tell him, "there would be one Star Wars movie, and it would only be fifteen minutes long."

Ajay nods. "Good point."

Outside, most of the houses and businesses we pass are already decorated for Halloween. In addition to a regular selection of skeletons, ghosts, witches, and carved pumpkins, a hundred different sidewalk scarecrows pose and leap and hang from every imaginable spot. Sidewalk scarecrows have always been a big part of the Cuper Cove Halloween festival. This year, quite a few of them hold signs that say MISSY FOR MAYOR.

More typically, for Cuper Cove anyway, a dozen hay-stuffed football players jog around the high school in full uniform. Downtown, a leather-jacketed scarecrow rock and roll band called Hay Ho Let's Go stands with guitars and a drum kit in front of Ramone's Barber Shop. At Saint Abigail's Church, where an entire sidewalk scarecrow wedding party marches up the front steps, we stop for Zoey Roy, who is in seventh grade with Ajay and me.

Zoey, a small, dark-haired white girl, moved to Cuper Cove at the beginning of last year. She wears cat's-eye glasses, black jeans, and anime T-shirts. Today, her shirt says GET IN THE ROBOT SHINJI. At lunch, Zoey sits at our cafeteria table and pours craft glue on her hands. She likes to let it dry and then peel it off for fun. Aboard the bus, she stops to stare at Mr. Beamon's hat. "That's no moon," says Zoey. "That's a space station."

Our bus driver taps his head. "It's too big to be a space station."

Zoey offers him a quick smile, then makes her way up the aisle to an empty seat in front of Ajay and me.

"I didn't know you like Star Wars," Ajay tells Zoey.

She gives a noncommittal shrug. "Star Wars is okay. Rom-coms are better."

From the look on Ajay's face, it's clear that he is clueless. So am I.

"Rom-com?" I ask.

"Romantic comedies," Zoey explains. "They're my favorite kind of movie. I watch them with my mom. She loves my dad, but she'd trade him in for Mr. Darcy faster than Inigo Montoya can say *Hello. My name is Inigo Montoya. You killed my father. Prepare to die.*"

I am still clueless.

"Who is Mr. Darcy?" says Ajay.

"Who is Inigo Montoya?" I ask.

"That's a lot to say if you really came face-to-face with the man who killed your father," Ajay points out.

Zoey shakes her head. "You guys are going to die alone."

Ajay shoots her a grin. "Inconceivable!"

For some reason, this makes Zoey laugh.

"Remember when Luke kissed Leia in *The Empire Strikes Back*?" Ajay asks. "Thinking about it now makes me want to throw up a little in my mouth."

The bus goes over a bump that nearly bounces us out

of our seats. Zoey shakes her head. "*The Empire Strikes Back* is not a romantic comedy."

"That might be why we like it," Ajay tells her.

"I bet you'd like *Romancing the Stone*," says Zoey. "Or *Splash*. *Groundhog Day* is a weird one, but it's still a rom-com. *Love, Simon* is surprisingly traditional. So is *To All the Boys I've Loved Before*. *Breakfast at Tiffany's* is always wonderful and *Sleepless in Seattle*, of course."

"Of course," I say, even though I have no idea what's keeping people awake in Seattle.

"And did I mention *Shrek*?" Zoey asks. "Everybody loves *Shrek*."

"*Shrek* is a romance?" says Ajay.

Zoey's eyes go wide. "Do you even have a heart?"

"We're in seventh grade," says Ajay. "We don't do romance." He nudges an elbow into my ribs. "Unless it involves Natalie Flores Griffin."

"Shut up," I tell him.

Zoey turns all the way around to face us. "I loved Natalie Flores Griffin in that movie with Bruce Willis."

Ajay shrugs. "I don't know that one."

"*The Wall and the Flower*," I say, because Ajay wasn't kidding. I really have seen every Natalie Flores Griffin movie ever made.

"That was her first big role," says Zoey. "Bruce Willis plays The Wall, a washed-up professional wrestler, and

Natalie Flores Griffin is a little girl who is The Wall's biggest fan. But then you learn that Natalie is actually Bruce Willis's long-lost daughter, and she's trying to get her parents back together. At the end, she's the flower girl at her own parents' wedding. Total rom-com, and it made Natalie Flores Griffin a star. Did you know that she's from around here?"

"Oh," says Ajay. "Is she really?"

"What part of 'shut up' do you not understand?" I ask him.

"How's this for a rom-com?" Ajay says to Zoey. "Danny just asked Natalie Flores Griffin to be his date for the Halloween festival dance."

"How did you do that?" Zoey asks me.

"He sent her an email," says Ajay.

Zoey tilts her head and narrows her eyes. "You sent an email?"

"Actually," says Ajay, "my sister's the one that sent the email, but she sent it from Danny's phone."

"That's it?" Zoey asks.

I shrug.

"You need more than an email before you've got a rom-com," Zoey says.

"Sorry," I say, even though I have no idea what I'm apologizing for.

"The Halloween dance could work," she offers, "but

it's probably a little too on the nose. Plus, you're missing a 'meet-cute.' You've got to have a meet-cute."

I understand all of Zoey's words, but her sentences are total gibberish. I look to Ajay for help. He's got nothing.

"What is a meet-cute?" I finally ask.

"Here's how your basic romantic comedy works," Zoey explains. "You open by describing the main characters' problems. Maybe there's a girl trying to choose a career instead of love, but nobody takes her seriously at work. Maybe there's a boy who's depressed because his fiancée left him at the altar to run away with the circus. Not only that, the old girlfriend took the dog."

"This is a comedy?" says Ajay.

"Next comes the meet-cute," Zoey continues. "That's when the couple who will eventually fall in love meet for the very first time. It's usually something clumsy and adorable, but for some reason, they don't get together. But we all know that they should."

"Danny and Natalie met in preschool," says Ajay. "In kindergarten she grabbed his juice box and squeezed so hard that fruit punch shot up his nose and squirted out of his eyes. It looked like he was crying blood."

"That was not cute," I say.

"It was more like a horror movie," Ajay recalls.

"So you've known each other since preschool," Zoey says. "We could work with that. But then you have to add a bunch of complications that force your characters to make one bad decision after another. Do you have any complications?"

"My mom is running for mayor," I remind her.

"Do you want her to win?"

"Not really," I admit.

Zoey nods thoughtfully. "Now we're getting somewhere."

"Exactly when do the funny parts kick in?" asks Ajay.

Zoey ignores him. "Eventually the complications have to lead everybody to some point of no return. It's got to be a real dark night of the soul that will force people to choose between two competing goals. Usually love wins out. But not always."

"This sounds like a total laugh riot," says Ajay.

Mr. Beamon steers the bus through a hard left turn. Zoey nearly tips off her seat, but she regains her balance. "In the end," she tells us, "everybody has to sacrifice something. Everybody loses, but it is a joyful defeat because somehow there will be an opportunity to find true love."

"My sister watches these kinds of movies," says Ajay. "Now I understand why she's always crying at the end."

"But it's totally worth it," says Zoey.

"Because of all the comedy?" says Ajay.

Zoey reaches across the back of her seat and gives Ajay a poke. "Because of all the love."

"Hey!" Ajay rubs his chest. "You're stronger than you look!"

Mr. Beamon taps on the brakes, and we slow to a stop in front of Cuper Cove Middle School. Everybody stands to gather books and bags and then heads for the door. "Do all those movies really work the same way?" I ask.

Zoey lifts a rainbow-colored My Pretty Pony backpack over her shoulder. "That's the basic formula."

"What's so interesting about them if they're all the same?"

"What's so interesting about life?" Zoey asks. "We're born, we do a bunch of stuff, we die. The end. It's all basically the same."

"That's not what we believe at my house," says Ajay.

"What do you believe?" Zoey asks.

"We're Catholic," Ajay tells her.

"So you've got Jesus and the saints and all that?"

Ajay exits the bus after Zoey. "Jesus and the saints and we get to go to heaven if we don't make our mothers too angry."

Just before I follow, I remember why I rode the bus today in the first place. "I'll catch up later," I call after my friends. I turn back to Mr. Beamon. "I have something for you."

"Oh?" he says.

I reach into my bag and retrieve the coffee cup with

Mom's business card. "My mother says you might sell your house. She wants you to have this."

Mr. Beamon leans forward and reads the message on the side of the mug. "Everything turns to sold, huh?"

"That's what happens when you're the top real estate agent in Cuper Cove."

Mr. Beamon nods thoughtfully. He and my mom grew up together. I'm pretty sure they might have dated once upon a time. Now he plucks a tiny green figure off the dashboard and drops it into the cup. "You can give that back to your mother."

From the bottom of the mug, a plastic toy that resembles a fat green jelly bean with a smiley face and a zucchini-shaped nose stares up at me.

"That's Mr. Nosey," Mr. Beamon explains.

"Mr. Nosey?"

He nods. "Please tell the mayor that if she'd like to stick her nose in my business, then she should call me herself."

"Mr. Beamon," I say after a long moment, "my mom sticks her nose into everybody's business. That's what she does."

"In that case," he says, "I look forward to her call."

Chapter 4

how to survive falling down a well

Barely twenty-four hours later, every single kid at Cuper Cove Middle School seems to believe that Natalie Flores Griffin and I are "a thing."

In the hallways, boys I don't know clap me on the back. In between classes, girls I've never talked to let me know how much they're looking forward to seeing Natalie and me at the Halloween dance. I find several envelopes addressed to Natalie Flores Griffin tucked into my locker as if I could hand them to her myself.

At lunch, I join Ajay at a cafeteria table with our regular group of friends. I pull up a metal folding chair and sit beside him. "Is there anybody you didn't tell about Natalie Flores Griffin?" I ask under my breath.

Ajay looks up from a comic book. "I told Zoey on the bus. That's all."

A moment later, Zoey, who's wearing a T-shirt that says EVERYTHING IS GONNA BE DAIJOBU, takes a seat across from us and begins to unpack a brown-bag lunch. "I thought you were nice," I tell her.

"Sometimes I'm nice." She opens a plastic container filled with apple slices. "Sometimes I'm not."

I point at the kids around our table. "Why did you tell them about me and Natalie Flores Griffin?"

Zoey glances at our friends. At the moment, they're having a strangely in-depth discussion about the best way to survive falling down a well. Besides Ajay, there's Darius Bryan, a tall, lanky black kid who wants to change the name of our math club to the Cuper Cove π-rates.

Because Pi + rates = Pirates.

On the other side of the table, Billy Bennet, who's built like a wide, pale cement block, sits next to Madeline MacSweeney. She's a tiny white girl who reminds me of one of those small, pretty peregrine falcons that's got eagle eyesight and a two-hundred-mile-per-hour attack speed. Mr. and Mrs. MacSweeney volunteer on my mom's campaign committee, so Maddie's got several MISSY CONSTANTINO FOR MAYOR buttons pinned to her backpack. I do not.

"If you fall down a well," Billy insists, "you should just wait at the bottom and yell for help."

"And what if nobody comes?" Maddie asks him.

Billy shrugs. "Take a nap and wait."

Maddie rolls her eyes. "Take a nap and die is more like it."

"See," I say to Zoey. "They're all cuckoo for Cocoa Puffs, but you still went ahead and told them and everybody else that I'm going out with Natalie Flores Griffin."

"Danny," says Zoey, "are you going out with Natalie Flores Griffin?"

"No!" I tell her.

"Then why would I say that?"

"How am I supposed to know?"

"If I fell down a well, I'd start counting," Darius announces. "If I stop falling before two, then I've probably hit water, and I can just swim to the top. If I get to five, I'm about four hundred feet below the surface of the earth, and that's going to be a problem. After ten, I'm over a thousand feet down, and I'm hoping this well goes all the way through the earth so that I can come out the other side."

"How long would it take to fall all the way to the other side of the earth?" asks Billy.

Darius scribbles a few numbers onto the cover of his notebook. "About three days," he finally says. "Not counting the time you lose bouncing and scraping off the walls on the way down."

"Wow," says Maddie. "Darius is a pi-rate and a spelunker."

I'm pretty sure she's being sarcastic.

"Here's the thing," Zoey says to me. She picks up an apple slice and points it at my face. "I didn't tell anybody about you and Natalie. Do you know why?"

"Why?"

"First of all, it's not my secret to tell." She takes a bite of the apple. "Second of all, it would cause complications. And every rom-com fan knows that complications are not supposed to happen before the meet-cute."

Ajay lowers his comic book. "I think the kindergarten juice box incident should count as Danny and Natalie's meet-cute."

Apparently, he was paying attention during the rom-com lecture Zoey gave on the bus yesterday.

"You can't put several years between meet-cute and the next step," Zoey tells him. "And before all that, we have to discover what our main characters really want."

"That's easy," says Ajay. "Danny really wants to go on a date with Natalie Flores Griffin. Next question?"

Zoey shakes her head. "It's got to be less obvious than that."

"Hey, Danny," Billy calls to me now. "How would you get out of a well?"

"I'd avoid falling in in the first place," I tell him.

He shakes his head. "It doesn't work like that."

"Maybe it works like that if you're lucky enough to be going out with Natalie Flores Griffin," says Darius.

I turn back to Zoey. "Okay, so how does everybody know about this?"

Zoey takes another bite of her apple. "So there's this

thing called the Internet. Sometimes it's like a phone booth where you can have private conversations. Other times it's a library where you can look up all kinds of information. And sometimes it's like one of those grocery store bulletin boards where people share messages for everybody to see about yoga classes and lost puppies."

"Why are you telling me about the Internet?"

"Have you gone online recently?"

I would if I could, but Asha's still got my phone. "No."

Zoey reaches into her lunch bag and pulls out her cell. We're not supposed to use our phones during the day, so she takes Ajay's comic book and uses it to disguise the fact that she's swiping at a screen. It's a good thing none of our teachers are nearby, because Zoey is about as subtle as a firecracker at a funeral. A moment later, she closes the comic, places it atop the phone, and slides everything across the table to me. "Check it out," she tells me.

I glance around before I take the book. It's a weird Archie horror issue called *Jughead: The Hunger,* and it's more likely to attract a teacher's attention than a phone. Finally, I lift the cover and glance at Zoey's cell. On-screen, there's a pretty Instagram selfie of a smiling Natalie Flores Griffin.

"Look at what she wrote," Zoey tells me.

I lean forward and read the caption.

I JUST RECEIVED THE BEST NOTE EVER. MAY BE I'M GOING TRICK-OR-TREATING WITH MY FAVORITE BOY NEXT DOOR! THANKS, @DANNYCONSTANTINO!

"Teacher coming," says Darius.

Zoey grabs her phone and slips it back into the lunch bag. Ajay takes *Jughead: The Hunger*, slides it between the pages of a notebook, and then heads to a lavatory, where he'll probably hide—and read—until the end of the period. Meanwhile, I feel like I have been punched in the stomach.

Nearby, a boxy intercom speaker attached to the wall buzzes to life. There's a squeal of feedback followed by my grandmother's voice, which fills the room. "DANNY! DANNY CONSTANTINO! COME TO THE OFFICE! RIGHT NOW!"

"Now what?" I say.

"You better go find out," says Billy.

Like all my friends—like the whole school, really— Billy both loves and fears my grandmother.

I stand, gather my things, and head for the door. "We can't wait to meet your date!" Darius calls after me.

I turn and shout at the top of my lungs. "NATALIE FLORES GRIFFIN IS NOT COMING TO CUPER COVE!"

A sudden wave of quiet washes across the cafeteria and stops me in my tracks. I scan the room and see every face staring back. A small girl with curly red hair gets to her feet and takes an unsteady step. She looks as if she's about to burst into tears. "She's not?"

I stare at the kid for a moment, then shake my head. "No."

"Why not?"

I have no idea what I'm supposed to say.

"What happened?" asks the girl.

"Nothing happened," I say. "It's just—"

"Did you break up?"

I shake my head. "It's not like that."

"Is she sick?"

"That's it," I say. "She wants to come, but she's sick."

Another screech of feedback interrupts our conversation. Gram's voice explodes from the intercom once more. "DANNY CONSTANTINO. WHERE ARE YOU? GET TO THE OFFICE RIGHT NOW!"

"I've got to go," I tell the redheaded girl.

She takes a quick step forward and grabs my hand. "Please tell Natalie that we're praying for her."

This, I realize, is what it must feel like to fall down a well.

"Sure," I say.

"Promise?"

"You bet." I pull my hand away and get out of the cafeteria as quickly as possible.

A moment later, I step into our school's main office.

I'm surprised to find Ajay's sister, Asha, standing next to my grandmother's desk. "What are you doing here?" I ask.

Asha gives me a big grin. "I have your phone."

"I know," I tell her.

"And Danny," she says.

"Yeah?"

"Danny!"

"What?"

Asha bobs up and down on the balls of her feet. "DANNY!!!"

I glance over Asha's shoulder and see my grandmother laughing and shaking her head.

"What's going on?" I ask.

"Well," says Gram, "if Asha Kalli is telling the truth—"

Asha starts hopping up and down. "I am! I really am!"

"Danny," says Gram, "you've got a date for the Halloween festival dance."

Chapter 5

natalie flores griffin is doomed

A huge, hand-painted version of Cooper the Unicorn covers an entire wall inside the Cuper Cove Middle School office. A speech bubble above Cooper's head holds the school motto so it looks like our mascot is yelling *UNICORN PRIDE IS JUSTIFIED!* On the day you learn you'll be going to the Halloween dance with Natalie Flores Griffin, it should be hard to disagree. But PRIDE is not what I am feeling right now.

TERROR is what I am feeling right now.

I stumble toward a chair near Gram's desk and drop into the seat. Thanks to my grandmother, tall ferns, potted peace lilies, and a couple giant yuccas fill the office. She's got a lush indoor garden at home too. According to Gram, there are two kinds of people in the world: anthophiles and dunderheads. I had to look up both words.

Anthophiles are people who love flowers.

Dunderheads are schmoes, schmucks, nitwits, and numbskulls.

Gram has strong opinions about flowers.

Now my grandmother is laughing, and Asha's still talking. "I saw Natalie's post on Instagram," she says. "I know I shouldn't have, but I went ahead and checked Danny's email."

"How did you open my phone?" I ask. "It's password protected."

Asha rolls her eyes. "JACKOLANTERN. I got it on the first try."

The whole neighborhood knew Jacko when he was alive. He wasn't a very sneaky dog then either.

"When I read what she wrote, I just couldn't believe it! I came over as fast as I could!"

"It's a good thing you don't have school today," says Gram.

Is it? I wonder. Is it really?

Asha turns to me. "Danny, Natalie can't wait to see you! She sent her phone number too."

Nearby, our principal, Mr. Maggio, in a cream-colored suit and thick-framed eyeglasses, reads lunchtime announcements into a heavy silver microphone. Mr. Maggio's voice, a deep, booming roll of thunder, echoes through hallways and classrooms. According to our principal, the chess club meeting has been canceled, there's a Girl Scout car wash this weekend, and a Halloween-themed cupcake sale is scheduled for next week. Even on a normal day, none of this would matter to me. But this is not a normal day. BECAUSE NATALIE FLORES GRIFFIN IS COMING!

"Can you believe this?" Asha squeals. "Can you believe this?"

Mr. Maggio shoots Asha a dirty look.

"Sorry," she whispers, "but Danny Constantino's got a date!"

"And for today's final announcement," Mr. Maggio says into the microphone. "Danny Constantino's got a date."

"Was that really necessary?" Gram asks as Mr. Maggio returns the mic to its shelf.

He gives Gram a big smile. "Principals need to have a little fun now and then too."

I am so glad I could be here for him.

Gram turns to me. "So what do you have to say for yourself?"

I say nothing because I have lost the ability to speak. Meanwhile, my mind fills with memories of me and little Natalie. In preschool, we used to share finger paints. In kindergarten, she used to hoard all the red LEGO blocks. In third grade, we realized that we both hated fish sticks. We'd sneak fish sticks out of the cafeteria and give them to squirrels at the edge of the playground. I wonder if Natalie is still a fish stick hater. And what if she's still a juice box squeezer too? What if she's changed and not for the better? Actually, what if I'm a bad person now, and I don't even know it?

"Danny!" Gram taps a pencil on the top of my head. "What's going on in there?"

I blink. "My life is flashing before my eyes."

"That only happens when you die," says Gram.

"I think I'm going to die."

"Sorry, Danny," says Asha. "Death is not one of your options."

I turn in my seat. "Here's something else that's not an option. I am not going on a date with Natalie Flores Griffin."

"What do you mean?" Asha says. "You're the one who asked her."

"No," I remind her. "YOU'RE the one who asked her."

"I know." Asha clasps her hands together and starts jumping up and down again. "And she said yes!"

"Then *you* take her to the dance!"

Before Asha can reply, the door swings open and now Ajay's here too. "I was on my way to class," he announces. "I look into the office, and I see my sister." He turns to Asha. "What are you doing here? Is everything okay?"

"Danny doesn't want to take Natalie Flores Griffin to the Halloween dance," Asha explains.

"Yes, he does," says Ajay.

"No," I say. "I don't."

Ajay gives me a dumbfounded look. "Then why did you ask her?"

I don't mean to raise my voice, but I can't help it. "I didn't ask her!"

The yelling attracts the attention of Mr. Maggio, who's now at the copy machine on the other side of the office. "What is all the hollering about?"

"Nothing!" I say.

"Natalie Flores Griffin!" says Asha.

Mr. Maggio smiles. "I loved her in *The Wall and the Flower.*"

"I liked her better in *Mutant Zombie Soul Pirates,*" offers Ajay.

"Wasn't that a cartoon?" Gram asks.

"She was still really good," says Ajay. "And very brave too."

"How could she be brave in a cartoon?" says Mr. Maggio.

Ajay rolls his eyes. "She had to fight mutant zombie soul pirates!"

Our principal nods. "That makes sense. Did you know that she's from around here?"

"Oh," says Ajay. "Is she really?"

"Yes!" shouts Asha. "And Danny doesn't want to take her to the Halloween festival dance."

"It doesn't matter what Danny wants," Ajay tells his

sister. "Natalie Flores Griffin is not coming to Cuper Cove."

Asha shoves my phone into her brother's hands. "Read this."

Ajay glances at the screen. A moment later, his mouth drops open. He looks at me, then down at the screen again. Finally, he turns back my way. "Danny," he says in an amazed whisper, "Natalie Flores Griffin is coming to Cuper Cove."

I nod.

"But she's Natalie Flores Griffin!" Ajay continues. "And you're—"

"Nobody," I say.

Gram taps me on the head with her pencil again. "You are not nobody."

"Natalie Flores Griffin is a superstar," I tell Gram. "She's supermodel pretty. She's super smart and super talented."

"And Danny's a super nobody!" Ajay shouts.

"Thanks," I tell my best friend. "Thanks a lot."

Mr. Maggio approaches us from across the room. "Am I hearing right? Is Natalie Flores Griffin coming to Cuper Cove?"

"It looks that way," my grandmother tells her boss.

Now Mr. Maggio is in shock.

"Natalie and Danny have been friends since pre-school," Gram adds.

"We haven't talked in a long, long time," I tell everybody.

"Danny," says Mr. Maggio. "This could be a very big deal for your mother's campaign."

"No," I say. "This has nothing to do with my mother."

Ajay nods thoughtfully. "I bet Natalie Flores Griffin could get a million people to vote for your mom, Danny."

"That would be a problem," says Gram.

"Why?" asks Ajay.

"Because then she'd be mayor," I say.

"Because there are fewer than ten thousand voters in Cuper Cove," Gram explains.

"Missy Constantino is a very strong supporter of public education," Mr. Maggio tells us. "A vote for Missy is a vote for Cuper Cove Middle School!"

Gram holds up a hand. "Wait a minute," she says. "This isn't some kind of stunt, is it?"

"What do you mean?" I ask.

Gram turns and speaks directly to me. "This isn't some trick to get a million people to pay attention to you for three seconds on InstantFace or SnapCracker or some other stupid thing?"

"Why would Natalie do that?" I ask.

"I'm not talking about Natalie." Gram looks at Asha and Ajay and then back to me. "I'm talking about you."

"No!" we all say together.

"Because Natalie Flores Griffin is a real person,"

Gram continues. "She might be famous, but she's a real girl. And Danny Constantino, you better be planning on taking her on a real date at the actual Halloween festival, including real dancing inside the Cuper Cove Middle School gym. Do I make myself clear?"

"Very clear!" I say even though I've never been on a real date, I don't know how to dance, and I have no idea what I'm talking about.

"Good," Gram says, "because that poor girl is going to be far from home, surrounded by strangers, and holding on to the arm of a boy who thinks pouring soda into a cup without spilling makes him debonair. It will probably be the scariest night of her life."

"Scarier than mutant zombie soul pirates?" says Ajay.

"That was the movies," Gram tells him. "This is middle school."

"And I bet this is your first date," Asha says to me.

"So?" I say.

Gram just shakes her head. "I love you, Danny. But Natalie Flores Griffin is doomed."

it's always now somewhere

I start the next day inside Gram's Camaro, which always smells a little bit like wet leather and motor oil. Not only that, the black vinyl on the dashboard is cracked, the radio doesn't work, and the seats are uncomfortable. At least once a week, Mom suggests selling it, but there's no way Gram is ever going to let go of this car.

"Did you talk to your mother about Natalie?" Gram asks as she accelerates through a yellow light.

"Not really." By which I mean not at all because I'm sure that Mom is going to launch into super-planning overdrive over this whole thing. She'll want to manage every aspect of Natalie's visit, including what we wear, where we go, what we eat, and who knows what else. She'll probably hire a photographer to follow us around and then use the pictures to attract potential home buyers to Cuper Cove. I can't even imagine all the ways she'll try to fit Natalie into the run for mayor.

Gram downshifts and then powers through a turn. "How did you manage that?"

I grab the armrest and hold on tight. "Mom worked late. I ate supper at your house. I did homework at Ajay's, and then I came home and went to bed."

"What about this morning?"

"I left the house early to ride with you."

Gram brings the car to a stop at another light. "So you've been avoiding her."

"That's my plan," I admit.

"For how long?"

"Four or five years?"

Gram sighs. "You realize that she probably already knows."

"You think?"

Gram starts revving the engine in anticipation of a green signal. "She probably knew Natalie Flores Griffin was coming before you did."

The light turns and Gram hits the gas. The Camaro's big engine roars like a troop of angry lions. "I'd like to try and keep the whole thing with Natalie kind of low-key," I shout over the engine.

"Then you might be hanging out with the wrong girl!" Gram hollers back.

I'm not sure if she's talking about Natalie, Mom, or herself.

I cross my arms over my chest, which is easy in the

Camaro because the seat belt does not include a shoulder strap. "I wish Mom didn't have to make everything such a big deal."

Gram lightens up on the gas and shifts into a long straightaway. "This is your first date ever, Danny. You're going with a Hollywood movie star. It's a big deal."

I close my eyes and take a deep breath. I guess it's too late to worry about it now.

Gram brings the car to a stop at a curbside spot across the street from our school building. She shuts down the engine and turns to me. "What does Natalie have to say about the whole thing?"

I don't reply.

"Have you talked to her yet?"

"Not yet," I admit.

Gram reaches across the seat and smacks me on the back of the head.

"What was that for?" I holler.

"There's a girl who says she's going to travel three thousand miles across the country to go to a dance with you, and you haven't called her yet?"

She reaches out to hit me again, but I duck out of the way. "I'll call her after school!" I promise.

"No," says Gram. "You'll call her right now."

"It's barely seven thirty in the morning," I point out. "And it's three hours earlier in California."

Gram shakes her head. "It's now in California. It's now here too. You're going to call her now."

"But—"

"She probably won't even answer. You can just leave a message."

"What if she does answer?"

"Tell her hello from Cuper Cove." Gram opens the door and steps out of the car.

"Where are you going?" I say.

Gram leans back into the Camaro. "Do you really want me to stay here while you call your date?"

"I guess not."

"Good choice." Gram closes the door and leaves me alone in the Camaro.

I sit quietly for a moment, then quickly pull out my phone and dial Natalie's number before I lose my nerve. It rings once. Twice. It's weird to think about a phone ringing somewhere near the Pacific Ocean because of something I'm doing just a few miles away from the Atlantic. The phone rings a fourth time. Fifth. I decide to hang up, but that's when a groggy voice says, "Hello?"

"Natalie?" I don't mean to shout, but then, she *is* very far away.

"Huh?"

"Natalie Flores Griffin?"

"Who is this?"

I try to get my voice under control. "Natalie? This is Danny Constantino . . . Good morning?"

"Danny . . . Danny from Cuper Cove?"

"That's me! Hi! Is this Natalie . . . um . . . also from Cuper Cove?"

I hear a low chuckle. "That's me. Do you know what time it is?"

I glance at the dashboard clock. "In Cuper Cove it's . . . now."

I get another laugh.

"Is it now there too?" I ask.

"It's always now somewhere." Natalie yawns. "But now here is four thirty in the morning."

"I know," I admit. "Sorry."

"Thanks for asking me to the dance," she says.

"Thanks for saying yes."

For a moment, there's an awkward silence between us.

"Everybody's excited to see you," I finally offer.

"I'm excited too," she says. "But please tell them all that I'm feeling fine."

"Huh?"

"I don't know why, but there's a whole bunch of Cuper Cove kids who think I'm sick," she explains. "They keep posting get-well notes and prayers for me online."

Note to self: Find that little redheaded girl.

"I can't believe you're coming to Cuper Cove," I say.

Natalie laughs. "Can I tell you a secret?"

"Sure."

"I came last year too. I love Cuper Cove, and I love Halloween. My aunt Jenny still lives in town. We come to Cuper Cove just so I can be normal for a little while. We made our own costumes, and then she took me trick-or-treating. I even went to the parade, but I stayed in disguise. I was LEGO Princess Leia."

"Why didn't you let me know you were here?" I say.

"Why didn't you call me before now?" she asks.

"Why did you stop emailing me?" I wonder aloud.

There's a long pause. "My parents got divorced," she finally says. "It happened about two years ago. I didn't want to talk to anybody for a while."

"Oh," I say. "That makes sense."

"It does?"

"I have no idea," I admit.

Natalie laughs again. "Do you still dress up for Halloween?"

"We make our own costumes too," I tell her. "Do you remember Ajay Kalli? Last year, he and I were a cow."

She laughs one more time. She has a really nice laugh. "A cow?"

"It seemed like a good idea at the time."

"Were you the front or the back?"

I decide to ignore the question. "This year we're going to build a giant cardboard unicorn."

"I'd like to see that."

"Do you want to go trick-or-treating with us?" I ask.

"Could we?" she says.

"Sure," I say. "Definitely."

"I'd like that. And the dance sounds like fun too," she adds.

"Can I tell you a secret?" I say.

"What is it?" Natalie asks.

"I don't know how to dance."

"That's okay," she says. "We'll figure it out." She hesitates a moment, then asks, "Are people at your school making a big deal about me coming?"

"They sort of are," I admit.

There's another pause. "Is that why you asked me?"

"No," I tell her. "I asked you because . . ."

I stop. The truth of the matter is that I did not ask her at all. In fact, I don't care about the dance. I don't really care about trick-or-treating either. On top of all that, I don't even care that Natalie is a movie star now.

"Because why?" she says.

"Because you're my friend," I blurt out.

There's a long silence before Natalie speaks again. "Danny," she finally says.

"Yeah?"

"That's a really good reason."

I'm just smart enough to know that I shouldn't speak right now.

"And Danny?" she says.

"Yeah?"

"It's still four thirty in the morning here. Can we talk later?"

"Okay," I say.

"Good. And Danny?"

"Yeah?"

"I'm glad you called."

"Me too."

Natalie laughs softly and then the line goes dead. Did I mention that she has a really nice laugh?

Chapter 7

unicorn pride is justified

By the time I get into the office, Gram's already dealing with a line of students, parents, and teachers who need her attention. I try to catch her eye, but she's too busy, so I decide to check back later.

"Mr. Constantino!" Mr. Maggio's big voice stops me in my tracks. "I've been thinking about you. Any word from our friend Natalie?"

I shoot a look at Gram, who glances up and gives me one quick shake of her head.

"Not yet," I tell the principal.

Mr. Maggio crosses the room and pats me on the back. "I spoke to your mom. She let me know that Natalie Flores Griffin can sit with the festival judges at this year's Halloween parade."

That's news to me. "There are actual judges?"

I thought the costume contest winners were simply picked out of a hat.

"Of course," says Mr. Maggio. "Did you think that we just picked winners out of a hat?"

I offer my principal a hearty laugh. "Pick winners out of a hat? That's the most ridiculous thing I've ever heard!"

"Right?" says Mr. Maggio. "The festival committee will have to approve it, but your mother has also suggested that Natalie can serve as a celebrity judge with voting privileges this year."

"Of course she did." I wonder if I can send Mom to South America or maybe lock her in a bank vault until after Natalie leaves. "I'm sure she'll tell me all about it when I get home."

"And Danny," Mr. Maggio continues, "we'd love to have Natalie Flores Griffin as part of our annual Cuper Cove Middle School Halloween pep rally too."

The Cuper Cove Middle School Halloween pep rally takes place the day before the downtown parade, so everybody comes to school wearing their Halloween costumes. It's supposed to be a regular day with regular rules, but it's difficult to expect sane behavior when half the school is dressed like some version of Satan.

"The pep rally can be a little overwhelming," I suggest.

"Don't be ridiculous," says Mr. Maggio. "Miss Flores Griffin will have so much fun that she'll wish she never left Cuper Cove in the first place."

I guess anything is possible.

"When you think about it," he tells me, "she could be just another kid at our school. If she were here, you and Natalie would probably sit next to each other in class. Maybe you'd even be going to the dance together."

"Maybe," I say. "But maybe not."

Mr. Maggio nods thoughtfully. "You're probably right. Lucky for you Natalie's not here after all."

Thank you. Thank you very much.

Just then, the school bell rings to start the day. "You better go," says the principal, "or your grandmother might give you detention."

I look toward Gram's desk. She's on the phone now, but she covers the receiver and whispers at me, "Come back at lunch!"

I nod, then leave the office and head down the hall as quickly as possible. I stop at my locker and put my backpack away. Meanwhile, I can't help wondering what it would be like if Natalie really had stayed in Cuper Cove. I bet we'd still be friends. I'm sure I'd want to ask her to the Halloween dance. I wonder if I would get up the nerve to do it in person. I suspect that the answer is no.

The morning goes by quickly, but I'm still exhausted by the time my lunch period arrives. I never realized being a celebrity would be so much work. First, everybody wants me to tell them about Natalie. Second, everybody wants me to hear their story about meeting someone famous. Finally, everybody cares a lot more about Natalie Flores Griffin than they do about Danny Constantino.

Thankfully, Gram is alone when I get to her office. She tapes a note to her computer screen, then turns to me. "Did you call your date?" she asks.

I nod. "I called."

"Did you talk?"

"We talked."

"And?"

I can't keep from smiling. "She's nice."

"Of course she's nice. You were that girl's best friend."

"She was friends with everybody," I remind my grandmother.

"That might be how you remember it," Gram tells me. "That's not how it was in real life."

"What do you mean?"

"Natalie Flores Griffin was a little ticking time bomb. Her parents were struggling at home. Natalie was acting out at school. Actually, she was acting out everywhere. They signed her up for every club, class, and sport they could think of to burn off all her energy. I remember her in dance, soccer, theater, gymnastics, swim club, wrestling . . ."

"Wrestling?"

Gram laughs. "The coach made her quit."

"Because she was a girl?"

"Because she was crushing everybody."

I sit at Gram's desk and pull a peanut butter and jelly sandwich out of my lunch bag. "They made her quit because she was good?"

"No." Gram reaches over and takes half of my sandwich. "They made her quit because she would beat her opponents and then sit on their heads and bounce up and down until they cried. She was literally crushing everybody."

I bite into my sandwich. "But Natalie was so nice."

"She was nice when she was with you," Gram says through a mouthful of peanut butter and jelly. "You two were just good chemistry."

We eat the rest of the sandwich without speaking.

"Have you told anybody about your call?" Gram finally asks.

I shake my head. "No."

"Then don't."

"Why not?"

"People were going crazy when this was all just a rumor. How's it going to be now that it's real?"

"I don't know," I admit.

"You're going to find out soon enough," she tells me. "Try to keep it for yourself a little while longer."

Somehow, I make it to the end of the day without

sharing my secret. I move in and out of classrooms quickly. I don't hang around in the hallway, and I skip the bus so I can ride with Gram. Mom's still at work when I get home, so I grab a snack and then start my homework at the kitchen table. I'm interrupted by a loud knock at the back door. Before I can answer, Ajay lets himself in.

"We're in my garage working on the unicorn," he says. "Are you coming?"

"Now?"

"Trojan unicorns don't build themselves, Danny."

I close my books and follow Ajay. Just a few minutes later, we're inside the Kallis' garage, which is more like a storage unit than a place to park cars. In fact, I can't remember ever seeing a car in here. Together, we step over a stack of old cardboard and scrap wood that's piled on the floor. At the back wall, several beat-up bicycle wheels lean against a worn wooden workbench that's covered with tools. "What are the wheels for?" I ask.

"They roll," says Ajay.

"Thanks." I nudge a giant box with my toe. "What about this?"

A side flap bursts open, and Zoey pops out. "Hi, Danny."

Startled, I leap back, stumble, and fall into Ajay.

Zoey stands, then nods toward the big carton she just crawled out of. "To answer your question, that's a refrigerator box."

I look up at Ajay. "Zoey's here."

What I really mean is, What is Zoey doing here?

"She's going to be a huge help," Ajay promises.

"My father is Jimmy Roy," says Zoey. "He owns Jimmy Roy Appliance World."

I think this is supposed to mean something to me. Unfortunately this means nothing to me.

Just then, Asha enters from a door that connects the Kallis' garage to their kitchen. "Is it true?" she asks Zoey. "Are you an endless supply of cardboard?"

"It's true," says Zoey. "I am."

Now I understand.

Asha claps her hands together. "We're going to have an endless supply of cardboard!" Her tone suggests that cardboard is worth its weight in diamonds. For our purposes, she might be right.

"I've been meaning to ask," I say. "How exactly are we going to make a unicorn out of cardboard?"

"Show him," Ajay says to Zoey.

Zoey reaches into a pocket and pulls out a wrinkled piece of notebook paper that's been folded into a palm-sized rectangle. She opens the sheet, stretches it flat, and holds it so I can see a stunning pencil sketch of a wild, graceful unicorn galloping through a lush, misty forest. "Did you makes this?" I ask.

Zoey offers a little shrug. "I like to draw."

I stand. "It's amazing."

"That's why I asked her to help," says Ajay. "She's an artist."

"Plus I bring an endless supply of cardboard," Zoey adds.

"That's pretty good too," says Asha.

I look at the boxes piled around us. "Do we really need all this?"

Asha lifts a big appliance carton. "We'll probably need even more. Cooper the Trojan Unicorn is going to be huge."

"Big enough to carry at least two people inside," says Zoey.

"We'll dress up like ancient Greek warriors," adds Ajay. "We can pull Cooper in the pep rally and in the parade."

"Who gets to ride inside?" I ask.

Ajay, Asha, and Zoey exchange a quick glance. "Natalie Flores Griffin," they all say at once.

"Oh no," I say. "Natalie is not—"

Ajay cuts me off. "Just think about it. Everywhere Natalie goes will turn into a mob scene. She won't get to see the parade. She won't have any fun, and we'll hardly get to talk to her. This way, we can all go to the parade together. Maybe the pep rally too."

"You want to put her inside Cooper the Trojan Unicorn?" I say.

Ajay grins. "Isn't that what a Trojan unicorn is for?"

I study the materials spread around the garage. "It's really going to be that big?"

"We have an unlimited supply of cardboard," Asha points out.

"And this definitely won't be like the cow?"

"The unicorn is a much more graceful creature than the cow," offers Zoey, who pauses, then adds, "Nothing against cows."

I think about Natalie going to last year's parade in disguise, and I consider my own limited celebrity experience at school. I can see why staying undercover—or inside a unicorn—might make sense. "Okay," I say. "You're right. This is a great idea."

Ajay smiles. "I stole it from Odysseus."

I take the unicorn drawing from Zoey. "May I?"

She shrugs. "Sure."

I find a hammer and a stray nail among the jumble of tools on the work bench. A couple whacks later, I point at the paper now hanging on the wall. "Unicorn pride," I tell my friends. "It's justified."

For the next hour or so, we break down boxes and spread them flat. With duct tape, staples, and a few long, slender pieces of wood for extra support, we connect pieces of cardboard so that we make large rectangles that stretch the length of the garage floor. Standing on edge, they'd touch the ceiling. Zoey kneels atop one of the rectangles and begins to sketch the outline of a horse's body that will be slightly bigger than a minivan.

"What about a horn?" I ask.

"That will come later," Asha promises.

While Zoey and Asha draw, Ajay and I try to figure out how to attach wheels to a sheet of plywood so that our Trojan unicorn can move atop a rolling platform. Without a bicycle's forks, it's going to be a challenge. Still, when Ajay steps back to consider the work in progress, he announces, "This is awesome."

Zoey, pencil between her teeth, laughs while she erases a bushy tail, which, at the moment, looks like a set of hot rod flames shooting out of a horse's butt. "It has potential."

The whole thing still looks like a pile of scrap wood and used appliance boxes to me. "Are you kidding?"

Asha lowers her own pencil. "Danny," she says, "you have to look past the mess."

Late afternoon sun shines through dirty garage windows. The light makes specks of airborne dust glow like diamond fireflies. I squint to pretend that those fireflies are floating and flickering above some magical unicorn glade. No matter how hard I try, I'm still standing in a garage filled with junk.

"Beginnings are supposed to be messy," Asha adds.

"Is that how this works?" I ask.

"That's how everything works." She finds her pencil and returns to drawing.

A half hour later, Zoey lets us know she's got to leave soon. "It's Wednesday," she explains. "I cook on Wednesdays."

"You cook?" says Ajay. "For what?"

Zoey rolls her eyes. "At my house, we call it supper."

Asha laughs. Ajay and I continue trying—and failing—to figure out some way to attach wheels to a sheet of plywood. Zoey grabs a marker and adds long, fancy eyelashes to our magical creature's face. I guess this unicorn is going to be a girl. A few minutes later, a big truck pulls into the driveway and honks a horn.

"That's my father." Zoey stands and considers the giant horse sketch covering the cardboard sheet spread across the floor. "What do you think?" she asks.

Asha, Ajay, and I study the drawing. "Not bad for a beginning," says Asha.

"She means it's excellent," says Ajay.

"That's what I said," Asha tells him.

Zoey smiles. "I think so too."

The sun is almost all the way down when I start home, so I walk around the block rather than cut through neighbors' yards. Approaching my house, I see Gram's Camaro in the driveway. In the shadows, the car looks like a big cat ready to pounce. A shadow paces back and forth across the kitchen window. Gram doesn't pace, which means Mom's home. I haven't seen her in over twenty-four hours. But the last twenty-four hours have been amazing, and I don't think she can take that away. I really believe that.

Until I open the door.

do not say shebang!

Inside, Mom's hollering at somebody, but she doesn't sound angry. I open the door and discover that she's yelling into the phone. "Roddy," Mom says. "Don't you understand? This changes everything!"

Gram's seated nearby with both shoes off and one foot on the kitchen table. She leans forward and massages her toes. "Hey, Danny. How was your day?"

It's hard to believe that I was on the phone with Natalie Flores Griffin less than twelve hours ago. "It had some good parts."

She flashes me a quick grin. "Glad to hear it."

Sometimes, when the light is just right and Gram's expression is just so—like right now—I can see exactly what she must have looked like when she was a girl. I am sure she was a troublemaker.

"Who's Roddy?" I ask.

"Roddy MacSweeney," says Gram.

"Madeline MacSweeney's father?"

Gram nods. "He's on the Halloween festival committee with your mother."

Mom is on so many community boards and town committees that I don't even try to keep track anymore. "What changes everything?" I ask.

"What do you think?" says Gram.

I glance at Mom, who's got a cell phone tucked between her head and shoulder. At the same time, she's stuffing chopped pineapples, blueberries, and bananas into a blender. "I'm making a power smoothie," she whispers to Gram and me. "Want some?" She adds a scoop of oatmeal and a package of frozen green spinach to the mix.

"Replace the spinach with a quart of mocha caramel ice cream, and then we'll talk," Gram tells her.

Mom responds by fastening the blender lid and pushing a button, which creates a sound that's nearly as loud as Gram's Camaro.

Mom turns her attention back to the phone. "Roddy," she shouts over the blender. "Listen to me! This is a once in a lifetime opportunity. A real live celebrity festival queen just fell out of the sky and into Cuper Cove. We're talking free publicity, TV coverage, social media, you name it . . . Yes, the whole shebang . . . SHEBANG . . . It means 'big deal' . . . You learn something new every day . . . Roddy, I need you to focus. The sun is shining. It's time to make hay . . . It's a saying . . . Never mind about the hay. Just call Alma Putski and tell her she can be our Halloween queen next year . . . I know how old she is . . . I know one hundred is a big birthday . . . Roddy, after ninety-nine all the birthdays are big, so I think we can agree that being Halloween queen at a hundred and one will be no less impressive than . . . Don't be a pessimist. Of course she'll be here next year . . . No, Alma will not think your call is a shebang . . . Roddy, do not use the word *shebang* . . . Roddy, I'm hanging up now . . . Give Alma my love."

Mom ends the call, shuts off the blender, and shakes her head. "Saint Monica, pray for us."

"Saint Monica?" I ask.

"Patron saint of those dealing with disappointing children," Gram informs me. I have a feeling she may have prayed to Saint Monica one or two thousand times herself over the years.

"I'm not disappointed in Danny." Mom lifts the pitcher. "But let me tell you about this Halloween fest committee. If a gift horse pooped a gold brick in their lap, they'd call in a parade clown to scoop it up and throw it away." She fills a tall glass with thick green goo. "Anybody want some smoothie?"

"It looks more like a sludgie," I say.

Gram eyes the mixture. "It looks like plant food to me."

Mom looks my way. "Danny?"

"I'm not a plant," I tell her. "And please tell me you weren't talking about Natalie Flores Griffin just now."

Mom takes a big gulp of the spinach oatmeal fruit brew. "Delish," she says, "and definitely fuel for a future marine."

"We already gave one boy to that gun club," Gram mutters. "They're not getting Danny too."

"Danny could do a lot worse than grow up to be like his father," Mom says.

Gram turns to me. "Sorry, Danny. Your mom says you have to die before you turn twenty-six."

"That's not what I'm saying," Mom tells my grandmother.

I have to agree. "Gram, that's not what she's saying."

"Danny," says Gram, "please tell my daughter that it looks like she just ate a caterpillar."

It's true. Mom's smoothie put a thick green mustache on top of her upper lip.

"Why don't you tell her yourself?" I ask.

Gram switches feet and starts massaging her other toes. "I don't want it to sound like all I do is criticize."

Mom takes a napkin and dabs her mouth. "So I was just talking to Roddy MacSweeney about Natalie Flores Griffin."

"No," I say. "She is not going to be the Cuper Cove Halloween queen."

Mom sips more spinach smoothie. "Why not?"

"We don't need a queen," I tell her. "We've got you."

"I'd rather run city hall than a royal castle," Mom says. "And by the way, I'd appreciate it if you'd pitch in a little more on my campaign."

"Your campaign to be home even less than you are now?"

"Danny," says Mom. "I'm doing all this for you."

"You're certainly not doing it for Alma Putski," says Gram.

Mom rolls her eyes. "If it makes you feel better, we'll give Alma a pumpkin and tell her she was the best Halloween queen we've ever had. She won't even know the difference."

"I didn't invite Natalie so you could make her your own celebrity apprentice," I tell my mother.

"Danny," Mom says, "from what I hear, you didn't invite Natalie to anything."

"What are you talking about?"

Mom lifts her glass, tips it back, and finishes the green power potion. She wipes her face and gives me a grin. "Asha sent that invitation, and then Natalie Flores Griffin fell into your lap."

"Excuse me," Gram says from her seat at the kitchen table, "but nobody will be spending any time in my grandson's lap."

I feel my face burn red. "How do you know who asked who to what?" I turn to my grandmother. "How does she know these things?"

Gram shrugs. "It's possible that she's a witch."

"It doesn't matter if I'm a witch or not," Mom says.

"So you're not denying it?" Gram asks.

"I am not a witch," Mom promises.

I'm not sure if I believe her.

"Even if I was a witch," she continues, "having Natalie Flores Griffin in town for Halloween and not asking her to be our festival queen would be rude. She's a celebrity. Actually, she's a big star. She's going to want to be in the spotlight."

I take a seat at the table across from Gram. "I happen to know for a fact that she does not want to be in the spotlight."

"It sounds like you and Natalie have discussed it," says Mom.

"That's right."

Mom brings her glass to the sink, gives it a quick rinse, and places it in the dishwasher. She does the same for all the pieces from the blender. "Did she tell you about her new movie?"

"We didn't talk about movies."

"It's called *Sidewalk Scarecrows*," Mom says. "It's all about a group of scarecrows in a small New England town during Halloween. Sound familiar?"

I shift uncomfortably. "So?"

"So she's in a movie that's totally based on our town, Danny. Do you really think she's coming to Cuper Cove to stay out of the spotlight?"

"I really think she doesn't want to star in any show that you're planning."

"I bet I can convince her otherwise," says Mom.

I stand. "Listen, Miss Everything-I-Touch-Turns-to-*Sold!* It's not up to you. It's up to Natalie, and she already made her decision."

Mom closes the dishwasher. She faces me for a moment, then turns to Gram. "Remember when Danny used to respect his mother?"

"I respect you," I say. "I just want you—"

"To do everything your way?"

"Only if I'm right." I don't mean to raise my voice, but now I'm kind of yelling. "Which I am!"

"I'll let you know when you're right," Mom says. "It hasn't happened yet."

"You're going to tell me what's right?" I ask. "You just stole a festival crown from a hundred-year-old lady, and you drank a spinach sludgie for dinner." I make a face and gag. "That's not even food!"

Mom closes her eyes and sighs. "Saint Monica—"

"I don't understand why you actually pray," I tell my mother. "You already think you're God."

"Maybe I just like talking to myself," Mom snaps at me.

"So your biggest fan won't have to miss a word you say?"

"Danny," says Mom, "if I were God, there'd be some serious smoting going on right now."

"Okay," says Gram. "That's enough. One of you is just acting like a monster right now."

"Even your grandmother thinks you're acting like a monster," says Mom.

"I never said which one of you is the monster," Gram points out.

"Fine." Mom turns to storm out. At the kitchen door, she stops and looks back. "We'll just leave it up to Natalie!" After the pronouncement, she stomps away.

Gram sighs. "She always was very good at the dramatic exit."

"This isn't fair," I say. "She's going to find a way to get what she wants even if she's the only one that wants it."

"Danny," says Gram.

"What?" I snap.

She points at a big canvas purse that Mom left behind. "Push that over to me."

I slide the bag across the kitchen table, then watch Gram rummage through my mother's stuff. "Do you think Missy wanted to give us money for pizza tonight?"

"No," I say.

Gram pulls a couple twenty-dollar bills out of Mom's bag. "And yet, that's exactly what she's going to do."

A quick Camaro ride later, Gram and I are eating thick sausage and mushroom slices at Angelo's Pizza. According to a set of pictures hanging above us, Presidents Obama, Kennedy, Nixon, and Carter have all eaten at Angelo's too. So have two popes, Amy Poehler, Dr. Seuss, Aerosmith, and several dozen Red Sox, Bruins, Celtics, and Patriots.

Across from us, one whole wall is dedicated to Cuper Cove's biggest star, Natalie Flores Griffin. Along with autographed photos, publicity shots, and newspaper clippings from *The Wall and the Flower* and *Mutant Zombie Soul Pirates*, there are posters of *Muzzy Fields*, starring Natalie Flores Griffin as Muzzy Fields, a girl who wants to play on her twin brother's Little League team, *Shake It Up!* starring Natalie Flores Griffin as Lilly Mercado, a girl who wants to be more than just a tambourine in her family's wedding band, and *Goodbye, Buster*, starring Natalie as a girl named Buster who lives with her grandfather, her great-uncle, and a very old dog.

Bring a box of tissues to that last one. I'm just saying.

Finally, over Angelo's bar, a set of framed photos hangs beneath a sign that says OUR REAL HEROES. My dad is there along with a dozen other Cuper Cove men and women who died in the military. I wish I knew what Dad might say about Natalie Flores Griffin, Alma Putski, Cooper the Cardboard Unicorn, and a thousand other things too. Instead, he hangs out inside picture frames while I try to make sense of everything without him.

In our booth, Gram wipes pizza sauce off her face, then leans across the table. "So," she says to me, "what have we learned today?"

I take a sip of root beer. "Angelo's pizza is lots better than a spinach sludgie."

"Everybody's pizza is lots better than a spinach sludgie," says Gram. "What else?"

I shrug.

Gram points at the pizza I didn't expect for supper tonight. "Not everything has to go your mother's way."

Chapter 9

i am now a chatface snapcracker virus

I ride to school with Gram on Friday because first, the Camaro. Second, Asha warned me that my name appeared on another one of Natalie's social media accounts this week. In the words of my grandmother, I am now a ChatFace SnapCracker virus. That's going to make it difficult to avoid that little redheaded girl.

"How did Mom know about Natalie's scarecrow movie?" I ask as Gram steers us past a house with a gigantic, inflatable spider perched on the roof. Like I said, Halloween is a big deal around here.

"I told you," says Gram. "Your mother's a witch."

"She's not a witch."

"She didn't deny it."

"Yes," I say. "She did."

"I'm not convinced." Gram roars around a pickup truck filled with fake skeletons. At least I hope they're fake.

"Mom probably just googled it."

Gram offers no reply.

"I mean about the scarecrow movie."

"I know what you mean." Gram plows through a pile of autumn dry leaves.

"And why do you think Natalie keeps posting things online if she wants to keep her visit to Cuper Cove a secret?"

"Did she say she wanted to keep it a secret?" Gram asks me.

I think back on our phone call. "I don't actually remember."

"Maybe you should ask her."

"I don't know," I say.

Gram glances my way. "Why wouldn't you just ask her?"

I turn and face my grandmother. "I don't want Natalie to feel like we don't want to see her just because she might have to do some publicity for a movie."

Gram puts on a signal and turns toward school. "So this is about Natalie's feelings?"

"I'm just saying—"

"Maybe you don't want to ask because you might not like the answer."

"No," I say. "That's not it. Because no matter what happens, I get to hang out with my friend Natalie."

Gram nods thoughtfully. "That's a very healthy way to look at things, Danny."

"I am a very healthy person," I tell my grandmother.

"So you'll be fine if you discover that Natalie's trip is actually just some kind of publicity stunt?"

"That's not going to happen."

I really hope that's not going to happen.

At school, Gram stops at the curb. She shuts off the engine and then sits quietly with both hands resting on the steering wheel. "Danny," she finally says, "you need to be ready for anything."

I think about this for a moment. "How can you be ready for anything?"

"As a matter of fact," says Gram, "you can't."

I don't even try to respond to that. "If you don't mind," I tell her, "I'm going to sit here and study for a little while."

"In the car?"

"We've got a math quiz today. If I stay here, I can look it over one more time without anybody distracting me."

Gram shrugs. "If you say so. Just don't be late."

I nod toward the round-faced clock on the Camaro's dashboard. "I'll watch the time."

Gram laughs. "The hands on that clock have been in the same place since before you were born." She removes her wristwatch and drapes it over the shift knob between our seats. Unlike Mom, Gram's got a watch that tells time and that's it. "Lock the car doors when you come inside."

I wasn't lying about the quiz. I should have studied more last night, but I spent a long time texting with Natalie instead. It strikes me that all of my study schedules, all of my Halloween plans, and pretty much every part of my life has been turned upside down because of Natalie Flores Griffin. And she's not even here yet.

I pull out my math book and try to solve a word problem involving a girl named Marlena who's got a large knife, an apple pie, and several hungry friends. It doesn't go well. But seriously, who thought it would be a good idea to give this girl a knife in the first place? After several false starts and a couple dead ends, I jot down 42 and hope for the best.

Looking up, I notice that there are a lot fewer people moving around outside now. I glance at Gram's wristwatch. Even though I'm sitting less than fifty feet from the school's front door, I am going to be late. I stuff my book into my bag, hop out of the Camaro, and race across the street. Before I reach the opposite curb, a sudden shriek of brakes and a foghorn blast of sound nearly knock me off my feet.

That's what happens when you step in front of a bus.

If you're lucky.

The big yellow school bus—which happens to be my

own big yellow school bus—comes to a stop about two feet short of running me down. Behind the windshield, Mr. Beamon gives me a hard stare. He puts his head on the steering wheel, and then he waves me over.

"Sorry," I say when Mr. Beamon opens his window.

"You okay?" he asks calmly.

I nod.

"You didn't look both ways before you crossed the street."

"I'm late for school," I explain.

"How about you look where you're going next time?"

"That's a good idea," I agree.

Mr. Beamon sighs, closes his window, and revs the engine. I step out of the road and onto the sidewalk, but before I can walk away, he reopens his window. "Danny," Mr. Beamon calls to me. "Are you really going to the Halloween dance with Natalie Flores Griffin?"

"Who told you that?" I ask.

"A bus driver hears things."

"You heard right."

"Then your mom will be especially happy I didn't kill you just now."

"What do you mean?" I ask.

Mr. Beamon raises an eyebrow. "You can't tell me that Missy Constantino is not trying to find a way to take advantage of a celebrity visit to Cuper Cove."

"You know my mom pretty well."

"A long time ago, Missy Constantino and I went to the Cuper Cove Middle School Halloween dance together. If I remember it right, the dance is a lot more fun if you're not dead."

"You and my mom," I say to Mr. Beamon. "Were you like—"

"We grew up together," he tells me. "She's always been one of my favorite people."

"Really?"

"Yes," Mr. Beamon says. "Really."

Behind me, the bell announces the start of a new school day. Mr. Beamon shifts the bus into gear. "You're late for class," he tells me.

"What kind of name is Shad?" I blurt out.

Mr. Beamon smiles a little. "I'll tell you about that another time."

I watch the bus pull away, then take a deep breath and head into the school building. Gram's waiting just inside the door. "Danny," she says sharply. "Where have you been?"

"I almost got hit by the bus," I tell her.

Gram crosses her arms. "But apparently it missed you."

"You say that like it's a bad thing."

"You were probably rushing and stepped into the street without looking."

"Something like that," I admit.

"I will celebrate the fact that you were not killed by sending you to class without detention."

First I dodged a bus. Now I've dodged a bullet. But apparently, that's not good enough for me. "Can I ask a question?" I say to Gram.

She puts both hands on my back and pushes me down the hall. "No."

"It's more like an observation."

"I don't want to hear it."

"I think Mr. Beamon likes Mom."

Gram stops pushing. "Why do you think that?"

I turn to face my grandmother, who is standing in front of a set of science fair posters hanging outside a closed classroom door. One especially colorful piece of artwork outlines a jelly doughnut's journey through the digestive system of a very large circus clown. Another shows a desperate-looking dog staring from the porthole of a rocket ship blasting away from the earth. I'm not sure if I feel more like the dog or the doughnut. Maybe I'm the clown.

"I could just tell," I say.

"One girl says she'll go to a dance with you, and now you're an expert on romance?"

I shrug.

"How did that even come up?" she asks.

"Mr. Beamon was pretty flustered from almost running me over."

"I wonder what he would have said if he hit you," Gram mutters.

Just then, Mr. Maggio rounds the corner. "Danny Constantino!" the principal calls from the opposite end of the hallway. "Just who I was looking for!"

Gram leans forward and whispers in my ear, "It looks like you were destined to get run over one way or another."

"Save me," I say quietly.

"Next time, don't be late." She turns and leaves me alone with Mr. Maggio, who I realize looks a lot like the clown on the science fair poster. I guess that makes me the doughnut.

"Danny," says Mr. Maggio, "I could use a Natalie Flores Griffin update."

"I think she's feeling much better."

Mr. Maggio looks confused. "Was she sick?"

"No," I say. "I mean yes. But not anymore."

"And what about our Halloween pep rally?"

"Pep rally?"

"Mr. Constantino"—Mr. Maggio tilts his head and looks down at me over his glasses—"did you forget about the pep rally?"

"I would never forget about the pep rally."

By which I mean I totally forgot about the pep rally.

"Will she be here for the big day?"

"I don't know," I confess.

"Danny," says Mr. Maggio, "what *do* you know?"

I glance up at the little rocket ship dog, who, if he could speak, would probably be saying EJECT! EJECT! EJECT!

"Mr. Maggio," I say, "I know that I am very late for class. Can I check in with you later?"

The principal sighs. "Far be it from me to tell a student that he should not go to class."

I turn and jog away before Mr. Maggio thinks of something else. "No running in the hallway!" he calls after me.

At lunch time, I catch up with my friends in the cafeteria. While we eat, I keep my back against the wall. Darius, Zoey, Billy, Ajay, and Maddie make a circle around me. For the most part, they keep our classmates' constant barrage of curiosity and questions away.

"We're really protecting you from yourself," says Darius. "If we left you alone, you'd eventually say something stupid. It would inevitably end up online, and then Natalie would be forced to cancel her trip."

"What could I possibly say?" I ask.

"There are more than one point five billion websites in the world," Darius informs me. "The possibilities are endless."

I turn to Madeline, who is sitting at my elbow. She's wearing a shirt that says VOTE FOR CONSTANTINO! "Where did you get that?" I ask her.

She shakes her head. "All of your mom's campaign volunteers have them, Danny."

"You're one of my mom's campaign volunteers?"

Just then, the redheaded girl that inspired me to lie about Natalie's health pops up from under our table. "Hi," she says from the floor.

"No comment!" I yell at her.

"What are you doing down there?" Maddie asks the girl.

"I just wanted to say that I'm really glad Natalie is feeling better," she says.

"What is your name?" I ask.

"Mira. It's short for Miroslava. It means 'peace and glory.' My dad says it also means 'light and ocean.' Maybe it means 'peaceful ocean'? Or 'glorious light.' I don't know exactly. Some people think I'm Irish, but my last name is Sergiyenko. After Ireland, Russia has the highest percentage of redheaded people in the world. Did you know that?"

This all comes out in one big rush.

I stare under the table for a moment. "I'll let Natalie know you said hi," I tell Mira.

Mira's face goes white. "You will?"

Maddie pokes me in the ribs. Hard.

I rub my side. "Sure. Is that okay?"

She starts to cry. "I was really worried."

I turn to my friends. Except for Maddie's willingness to puncture my lung when I say something stupid, they are no help. I lean back under the table. "Is there anything else?" I ask.

Mira shakes her head. "Thank you, Danny."

Maddie sticks her head under the table next to mine. "You can go now," she tells the small redheaded ocean of peace and light and glory.

Mira crawls away and Maddie turns to me. "Is it me, or is this getting weird?"

Chapter 10

use the horse, duke

After school, I sit in my room and focus on homework for a change. In math, we're graphing linear equations, which basically means drawing a bunch of straight lines. That's not too bad. Actually, I wish everything could be as easy as a straight line.

For language arts, I read a story called "Aschenputtel." It's an old and very creepy version of Cinderella in which the rotten stepsisters chop their own feet to bits and then get their eyes pecked out by pigeons. Of course, Cinderella still marries the prince and lives happily ever after. Weirdly, I think "Aschenputtel" might follow all of Zoey's romantic comedy rules.

Finally, I write a paragraph in my science journal describing what I think would happen to a freshwater pond if all the insects were to suddenly disappear. I'm not exactly sure of the answer, but I'm pretty certain it's not going to be good.

Once I finish with the damselfly apocalypse, I dig my phone out of my backpack and see that I've missed a call from Natalie. There's no voicemail. I can only think of a few reasons she would actually dial my number. Most of them involve having her phone in her back pocket. Just about everything else makes me worry that she's going to cancel her trip to Cuper Cove.

I glance around my room. Superhero movie posters cover my walls along with sketches of comic book characters I've drawn myself. I've definitely got some villains, but I mostly focus on the good guys. I think that's what my dad would like if he was around. And for better or worse, good guys don't act like jerks when their dates cancel. At least that's what I assume. I'm kind of making this up as I go.

I take a deep breath and then dial Natalie's number. The phone barely rings twice before she picks up. "Danny Constantino," she says without even a hello. "I was hoping you'd call back. Unless, that is, you're about to tell me you've changed your mind."

"Change my mind about what?" I ask.

"You and me going to the Halloween dance."

Before I can respond, a low, hollow *BOOM!* sounds behind Natalie.

"Where are you?" I ask.

"Have you changed your mind?" she says.

"No," I tell her. "Have you?"

"Absolutely not." She says this as if I've just suggested that she add cat fur to an ice cream cone.

"Great!" I say. "That's great."

"You sound surpris—" Natalie's cut off by two more loud explosions. *BOOM! BOOOOM!!!!*

"What's going on there?" I ask.

"It's a movie thing," she explains. "I'm not supposed to talk about it. But I can tell you that I think this scene relies a little too much on blowing stuff up."

Sometimes, drawing helps me to relax a little, so I grab a pencil and paper and start a quick sketch of the Batmobile. I'm apparently still on schedule to take a movie star to my middle school dance, so I need all the relaxation I can get. "I like movies where things blow up."

"Me too." Natalie lowers her voice. "But it's lots better when there's a story to go along with the fireworks."

BOOM!! BOOM!!! BOOOOOOM!!!!

I give the Caped Crusader a dark mask. "It sounds like you're getting shot out of a cannon."

"I'm not even in this scene. I'm just hanging out on set and doing my homework. I have to identify some key organisms that coexist as part of a California coastal habitat."

I think about my own homework. "What about insects?"

"Good one," says Natalie. "What would we do without insects?"

I wish I knew.

BOOOOOM!!!

"Is that why you called?" I say. "To ask about organisms?"

"I just wanted to talk," Natalie confesses.

"What do you want to talk about?"

"Anything," she says, "as long as it's not about any new movies connected to characters whose names rhyme with Marth Crader and Duke Frystalker."

"Marth Crader and Duke Frystalker?" Suddenly I'm shouting. "ARE YOU IN THE NEW STAR WA—"

"Can't talk about it, Danny."

"But—"

Natalie laughs. "Big fan, huh?"

I reach up and touch the homemade lightsaber sitting on a shelf above my desk. "Pretty big."

"Me too," Natalie admits. "One day, I'll tell you everything I know."

"But not today?" I ask.

"Nope."

I force myself to think about something else. "Everybody is talking about you at school," I tell her.

"What do they say?"

"Mostly they want to know if you're really coming to Cuper Cove."

"And what do you say?"

"Mostly nothing. It's none of their business."

"I'm glad you feel that way."

"Then why do you share online about coming to see me?" I blurt out.

There's a long silence before Natalie explains. "My mother wasn't going to let me go to the dance with you, Danny. But if I put it online and told the whole world . . ."

"Then she couldn't say no?"

"It worked this time."

"My mother would kill me if I did something like that."

"Mine too," Natalie confesses. "But I think it will be worth it."

I sketch a Bat-Signal in the sky behind Batman's car. "You really want to come all this way for a middle school dance?"

"You think it's weird that I accepted your invitation even though we're three thousand miles apart, we haven't talked in years, and the last time you saw me I was kind of angry all the time?" she says.

"It was a little bit of a surprise." I start feeling nervous about where this conversation might be going. "I didn't know you were angry back then."

Natalie laughs again. "That's why I said yes, Danny."

"What?"

"I had such a crush on you when we were in third grade."

"What?!" I say again.

"You are still the nicest eight-year-old boy I have ever met."

"I'm not eight anymore." I grab another piece of paper and begin sketching Batman in front of Gotham City's skyline.

"I bet there's a lot about you that's still the same."

"Like what?" I ask just in case there's anything about myself I need to change before Natalie arrives.

"When we were little," she tells me, "my parents used to fight all the time. They're friends now that they're not married anymore, but back then it was really kind of terrible. I think I tried to behave as badly as possible to make them feel as rotten as I felt. Does that make sense?"

I outline Batman's mask. "Sort of."

"It wasn't a good plan," she confesses.

"You were eight," I remind her. "Eight-year-olds aren't supposed to be good planners."

"I was a monster," she tells me. "Remember when I shot fruit juice up your nose?"

"I remember." I give Batman a cape and boots. "I also remember that I told you I didn't like it. Then you apologized, and you never did it again."

"You were so calm," Natalie recalls. "You were

supposed to pitch a fit or throw a tantrum, and that would have given me a chance to scream and cry and ruin everybody's day."

"Wow," I say. "You really were a planner."

"But you just wiped your face. And then you offered me one of your cookies."

"I was probably afraid of what might come next if I didn't share my dessert."

Okay. Not probably.

"Danny," Natalie says seriously, "you made kindness seem like an option. You made me think some kind of peace and quiet might be possible."

I stop drawing for a moment. "You thought all that when we were in third grade?"

"No," she admits. "But I've been thinking about it ever since."

"My grandmother says you used to wrestle kids to the ground and then bounce up and down on their heads until they cried."

"But thanks to you, I was trying to think kind and peaceful thoughts when I did it."

Rather than reply, I concentrate on sketching Batman's outfit which includes a utility belt that holds bat rope, bat grapples, batarangs, and of course an ultrasonic bat beacon because Batman without cool tools is just an angry white man in tights.

"I have a question for you," Natalie says now.

I nod even though she can't see me. "Ask away."

"You said you didn't ask me to the dance because of the celebrity stuff."

"So?"

"So the celebrity stuff comes with me whether you want it or not."

"I don't care," I say.

"You say that now."

"Is it really that bad?"

"Not every day," says Natalie, "but some days. It's easier around Hollywood. There's almost always some A-list personality just around the corner. Yesterday a group of ladies wouldn't leave my mother and me alone in the grocery store, so we told them Taylor Swift was in the produce section. The way they turned and ran, it was like we hit them with pepper spray."

"Was Taylor Swift really in the produce section?"

"I would never do that to Taylor Swift," says Natalie. "She's too nice."

"You know Taylor Swift?"

"Just a little. I was in one of her videos. She's been famous since before you and I were born, so it's not like we're friends, but she calls and checks on me now and then. She's more like a mentor."

I don't mention it, but if Taylor Swift is calling to check

on you, you might just be an A-list celebrity. In fact, if you look up *A-list celebrity* in the dictionary, I bet it says:

(noun): a person that Taylor Swift calls to check on.

"None of the celebrity stuff is really about me," Natalie continues. "People just like the stories I'm in and the characters I get to play. If it weren't me in those parts, it would be somebody else. The stories would be just as good. Maybe even better."

"I don't know about that."

"Either way," says Natalie. "I don't think most of those people really care about me. How can they? They don't even know me."

I think about Miroslava Sergiyenko, the little red-headed girl who looks like she's going to burst into tears every time she sees me at school. "I think some people care."

"Like you?" says Natalie.

"I wasn't talking about me."

Natalie does not reply, which makes me realize that I just said something really stupid.

"I was talking about your fans."

"So you're not a fan?"

Now I think she's teasing me. Either way, I don't think I'm helping myself here. "I mean that I am your friend. I would be your friend even if you were not a movie star. Also, you were awesome in *Mutant Zombie Soul Pirates*."

"You saw *Mutant Zombie Soul Pirates?*"

"And *Mutant Zombie Soul Pirates II: The Wreck-ening.*"

"Whoa," says Natalie.

"Friends see all their friends' movies," I tell her.

"Even when they're not good movies?"

"Especially then. Fortunately, all your movies are very good."

Natalie laughs. "You must like me a lot, Danny."

For a moment, I consider asking Natalie about the *Sidewalk Scarecrows* movie, but then I decide that it doesn't matter. Or maybe Gram's right, and I'm just afraid of an answer I'm not going to like. Before I can figure it out, we're interrupted by the biggest explosion yet.

"Are you all right?" I ask.

"It's Duke Frystalker," Natalie whispers. "He just used his horse to bring down a transport ship filled with Form Snoopers."

"His horse?"

Natalie lowers her voice to a ridiculous, deep bass. "Use the horse, Duke."

She's interrupted by an alarm bell ringing in the background.

"Are Marth Crader and Duke Frystalker about to have a kite scraber duel?" I ask.

"I have no idea what you just said," Natalie tells me, "but I think something just caught on fire."

"Really?"

"I should probably exit the building. Can I call you tomorrow?"

"I'd like that," I tell her.

"May the horse be with you, Danny."

The line goes dead. I glance down at the drawing of Batman. "Now what happens?" I ask him.

The Dark Knight says nothing. The ability to see the future is not one of the Caped Crusader's superpowers. Actually, Batman kind of stinks at relationships in general, so even if he could speak, he'd be useless.

I guess I'm on my own.

Chapter 11

total meet-cute

A week later, it's Saturday morning, and I'm in Ajay's garage sliding a utility knife along the outline of a big cardboard hoof. As it works out, building a Trojan unicorn out of cardboard and scrap wood is a lot harder than you might think. But after a few false starts and an unfortunate incident involving a sheet of plywood and Mrs. Kalli's minivan, we've got the project on track.

As I cut, I think back on the last few days. In school, kids continue to wait at my locker to ask about Natalie. Around town, strangers take my picture and then post photos online with hashtags like #NataliesDate, #NataliesBeau, and my personal favorite, #WhatIsSheThinking? Even Mom got flustered when a couple giggly teenagers showed up at our front door.

"Is Natalie Flores Griffin here?" a tall blond girl asked when Mom and I answered the doorbell.

"Why would Natalie Flores Griffin be here?" said Mom.

"We just want to say hi," explained the girl's companion, a dark-haired boy in an oversized Patriots jersey.

Mom turned to me. "Please handle this, Danny."

"You're the one who wants to be their mayor," I reminded her.

Mom studied the kids in the doorway. "Do you live in Cuper Cove?" she asked.

"Yes," said the girl.

"Are you old enough to vote?"

"No," said the boy.

Mom swung the front door shut. "Buh-bye."

"How do you put up with this?" I ask Natalie when we talk on the phone or text, which happens pretty regularly now.

"It's just part of my job," she explains.

"You're a thirteen-year-old girl," I point out. "You're not supposed to have a job."

"You're a seventh-grade boy," she tells me. "When did it become your job to have an opinion about what I'm supposed to do and not do?"

"That would be never," I admit.

According to Gram, growing up without a strong father figure makes it easier for a boy to recognize when he's wrong.

Of course, growing up with a strong mother figure isn't the solution to everything either. Mom has informed me, in no uncertain terms, that she intends to recruit Natalie to be our Halloween queen. For better or worse, Natalie's mother doesn't sound much better. "Your mom sells real estate," Natalie told me earlier in the week. "My mom sells me."

Mrs. Griffin is Natalie's manager. She works with agents and lawyers and various television and movie executives to make sure Natalie gets good parts and good money.

"According to my mother," Natalie told me on the phone, "I need to think of myself as a brand, a business, and a platform."

"What about actress?" I asked.

"Sometimes I think my main roles are cash cow and golden goose."

"I have experience if you ever need help with cow parts."

"I'm mostly vegetarian," Natalie told me.

"So?"

She laughed. "I avoid cow parts."

A sudden, sharp stinging sensation in my foot interrupts my thoughts. Looking down, I see that I've accidentally slid the utility knife off the cardboard and through the top of my sneaker. Asha, who is helping Zoey paint, points at my shoe. "Danny," she says, "I think you've got a problem."

Ajay stops pulling apart an old wheelchair in the

corner of the garage. He turns to see what's going on. I hear him gasp. "That looks like blood."

I stand, and pain shoots from my foot and up my leg. On a hunch, I glance at the utility knife still in my hand. Sure enough, a drop of blood clings to the end of the blade. "Uh-oh."

Ajay drops a wrench to the floor. "Put pressure on the wound!" he hollers in a voice that sounds several octaves higher than usual.

"How about you go into the house and get a bandage?" Zoey tells him.

"I will go into the house and get a bandage!" Ajay repeats, but he does not move.

"Shouldn't you go into the house?" I say.

"And get a bandage," Zoey adds.

"Right." Ajay sprints inside.

Zoey watches him run away. "Does he seem especially weird right now?"

Asha nods. "He can't stand the sight of blood,"

"Do you think he'll come back?" says Zoey.

Suddenly I feel very lightheaded. "Sure," I say, "but I might be unconscious by then."

"Lie down on the floor," Asha instructs me.

"What?"

"Just do it."

I lower myself onto the cold concrete while Asha

grabs an old folding lawn chair and places it in front of me. "Lift your foot onto the seat."

Dimly, I recall a first aid lesson from a couple summers ago. Billy Bennet's dad was our teacher. "When it comes to treating an injury, just remember RICE," Mr. Bennet told us over and over again.

RICE stands for *Rest, Ice,* something that begins with *C,* and *Elevate.*

"We're elevating the wound," I say to Asha.

She nods.

"I can't remember what the *C* stands for," I confess.

Asha unties my shoelaces and slides the sneaker off my foot. "I have no idea what you're talking about, Danny."

"RICE," I say.

"Ice?" says Zoey.

"That's the *I,*" I tell her. "What about the *C*?"

"I SEE a lot of blood," says Asha.

"That's not it."

"Keep your foot up."

I keep trying to remember the *C.* Is it *Cut? Coma? Convulsion?*

"We could use some bandages!" Asha shouts toward the door leading into the house.

Bandages do not begin with a *C.* "Cardiopulmonary resuscitation?" I suggest.

Asha grabs the utility knife that I dropped on the floor. "Don't move," she tells me. "This might hurt."

"What are you—"

She slips the sharp blade beneath my sock and makes a quick cut. A moment later, she peels a blood-soaked cloth away from my foot.

"Ouch!"

"We need those bandages!" Zoey shouts. "Stat!"

I lift my head and look at my bloody foot. "Stat?"

"They're always saying 'Stat!' on hospital shows," she explains. "I'm not exactly sure what it means, but it's like when somebody's been bitten by a poisonous snake, and they need the medicine immediately or else the patient will die. That's when they say, 'Get the anti-venom! Stat!'"

"It means immediately," Asha informs us.

"I haven't been bitten by a poisonous snake," I say.

"Good thing," says Asha. "Because Ajay definitely doesn't know the meaning of *Stat!*"

Zoey leans over and examines my foot. "You didn't hit an artery."

"How do you know?" I ask.

"Blood would be shooting out of your foot like a fountain. I've seen it in the movies."

"Just because it's in the movies doesn't mean it's true."

"Actually," says Asha, "the fountain-of-blood thing is true. But we should still put pressure on the wound."

I remember what the C stands for. "Compression!" I announce.

"I got this." Zoey grabs a strip of silver duct tape and a roll of paper towels. Quickly, she puts together a home-made bandage and wraps it around my foot while Asha and I watch.

"Nicely done," Asha tells her.

"I learned it from the movies," says Zoey.

"Is there anything you haven't learned from rom-coms?" I ask.

"Who said anything about rom-coms? I learned first aid from horror movies. Of course," she adds, "horror can be a lot like romances."

Despite the fact that I live in a town where Halloween is a bigger deal than Easter, Ramadan, and Chinese New Year combined, I do not enjoy horror movies. On the other hand, the duct-tape bandage on my foot suggests they might be useful for something.

"Of course," adds Zoey, "horror can be a lot like romances, but with murdering instead of meet-cute."

I think back on my language arts homework. Zoey and I are in the same class. "If 'Aschenputtel' were a movie, would it be rom-com or horror?"

Zoey nods thoughtfully. "It's got bloody mutilations, a charming prince, an evil stepmother, some eye-pecking pigeons, and a happily ever after ending. I'd say it's both."

"Things can be both?"

"Read *Dracula*," Zoey tells me. "Or how about *Bride of Frankenstein*? And let's not forget *Pride, Prejudice, and Zombies*."

"Who could forget *Pride, Prejudice, and Zombies*?"

"That's a romantic zombie comedy," Zoey tells me. "Also known as a rom-zom-com."

Before I can ask if rom-zom-whatever is an actual thing, Mrs. Kalli rushes into the room with Ajay right behind her. "Danny," says Mrs. Kalli. "What happened?"

Mrs. Kalli is a pharmacist at Cuper Cove Hospital. Ajay and Asha's dad works there too. He's some kind of heart doctor. I guess that's why the first aid kit in Ajay's arms is bigger than a small suitcase.

"Don't worry," Asha tells her mom. "It's just a flesh wound."

I try to sit up, but Zoey pushes me back to the floor. "Don't make me chop off that foot and eat it." She grins. "And thanks to the movies, I know how to do it."

I lie back down.

Mrs. Kalli kneels beside me and starts to peel Zoey's bandage away from my foot. "In general, I do not recommend duct tape as a treatment option."

"What's going on?" asks a familiar voice from the front of the garage.

I tilt my head back to see who's standing behind me in the open doorway. Even upside down, I recognize Mom and Gram. They're with a third woman I don't know. A fourth person, standing in bright sunlight, is nothing but a silhouette. I assume the two strangers are house shopping with Mom. She probably dragged them here when Ajay or Mrs. Kalli called to say I had an accident. After a week of being the center of attention, it would be nice if I could do one thing without an audience. "Nothing to see here," I call out. "It's just your basic self-inflicted knife wound. Please move along."

"That's funny," says Gram. "Because it looks like you're about to get your foot amputated."

"We don't have to amputate." I look up at Mrs. Kalli. "Do we?"

"We do not have to amputate," Mrs. Kalli promises.

"So you'll still be able to dance?" asks the silhouette.

"You're assuming he was able to dance before he stuck the knife in his foot," says Ajay.

"Why did you stick a knife in your foot?" asks Mom.

I don't answer because I just figured out the identity of the silhouette. "Natalie?"

"Hi, Danny," says Natalie Flores Griffin.

A little bit of twisting and turning gets me onto my elbows. I try to sit up, but I put too much weight on the lawn chair. It snaps shut on my foot like a bear trap.

"That must have hurt," says Gram.

I lie back on the garage floor. "A little bit."

"Are you okay?" Natalie asks.

I stare at the ceiling and pretend that my foot is not

exploding like a volcano made out of pain. "Totally fine," I say.

"Natalie and her mother got to your house just a few minutes ago," Gram tells me.

I nod, and with the folding chair still snapped shut over my ankle, I roll onto my side. I prop my head in my hand and give Natalie a big smile. "Welcome back to Cuper Cove."

Zoey leans against Ajay and whispers just loud enough for me to hear, "Total meet-cute."

Chapter 12

in time the savage bull doth bear the yoke

Zoey and Asha help me escape from the lawn chair while Gram makes introductions and Ajay runs back into the house to get me a new pair of socks. I'm sure he's just looking for an excuse to leave while his mom cleans up all the blood. Still, it is October, so I definitely appreciate the socks.

Mrs. Kalli presses something called a butterfly bandage to my skin, then helps me into a sitting position. "It was not as bad as it looked," she tells me.

"It looked very bad," says Ajay when he returns with socks.

"Not to worry," says Mrs. Kalli. "Danny will dance again."

"Only if you teach him a few moves first," Zoey tells Natalie, who hasn't said much yet.

"I've got moves," I say once I'm back on my feet.

My grandmother points at the collapsed lawn chair on

the floor. "We saw your moves, Danny." She turns and pats Natalie on the back. "Good luck, dear."

Natalie smiles. She's got a really pretty smile, plus dark brown hair and a soft, round face. Also, and I don't mean this in a bad way, her nose is bigger in real life than it looks on the screen. Actually, in real life she looks a lot more like I remember her than she does in the movies. I mean, she's definitely taller. She's also prettier than she was in fourth grade. Okay, who am I kidding? She's the most attractive person I've ever seen in my life. But at the same time, Natalie just looks like a normal seventh grader in jeans, sneakers, a denim jacket, and a T-shirt that says ANGEL CITY ROLLER DERBY.

"Can I help with . . ." She looks around the garage. "Whatever you're doing?"

"Sure," I say. "But what are you doing here?"

Suddenly, I'm on the receiving end of several dirty looks from both family and friends.

"I'm sorry," I say. "That didn't come out right. We didn't expect you till next week."

"But we're really glad you're here," adds Asha.

"Danny was going to say that," Ajay tells his sister.

"I was going to say that," I tell Natalie.

"The movie I'm on right now is either ahead of schedule or behind schedule," Natalie explains. "I'm not sure which."

"Do you mean . . ." I begin to ask.

"I can't talk about it," she reminds me. "Either way, the director let us go a few days early."

"We decided to come out and spend some extra time with my sister," adds Natalie's mom, who's wearing a heavy, rose-covered fleece over a pair of jeans and sneakers. Mrs. Griffin looks more like a pretty kindergarten teacher than a Hollywood mogul.

"And I wanted to come over and surprise you." Natalie shuffles her feet a little. "I hope that's okay."

"It's definitely okay!" I say. "And I am very surprised."

"In a good way," says Ajay.

"He was going to say that," Asha tells her brother.

"I was going to say that," I tell Natalie.

She gives me another smile. "This is lots better than talking to you on the phone."

Asha gets a big grin on her face. "You've been talking on the phone?"

"Almost every day," Natalie shares.

I feel my face burn red.

"When were you going to share this important piece of information?" Asha asks me.

"Yeah," says Ajay. "When were you going to share this important piece of information?"

"You guys," says Zoey. "Danny is not the kind of person who talks on the phone and tells."

I'm not positive, but I think Zoey means that as a compliment.

"Let's leave these kids alone," says Gram. "They'll be fine."

Natalie's mom glances at the blood-soaked sock balled up on the floor. "Are you sure?"

"Don't worry," says Asha. "I'll keep an eye on them."

This would be a lot more reassuring if Asha weren't still clutching a utility knife like a weapon. Not surprisingly, Mrs. Griffin appears reluctant to leave her daughter with a bunch of bloody strangers wielding sharp objects.

"I was just about to make myself a cup of tea," Mrs. Kalli says to Mom, Gram, and Mrs. Griffin. "Perhaps you would like to join me?"

Mrs. Griffin apparently decides that she'll be close enough to rush outside and save Natalie if necessary, so the adults head into the house. Once they're gone, Zoey points at Natalie's T-shirt, which shows an intense-looking helmeted girl with wings. "Do you like roller derby?" Zoey asks.

Natalie nods. "I'm in a junior league."

"Isn't roller derby kind of violent?" asks Ajay.

"Sometimes." Natalie shoots me a quick smile. "But I try to think kind and peaceful thoughts when I'm doing it."

Have I mentioned that Natalie has a really pretty smile?

"Do you want to see our secret project?" Ajay asks her.

"Am I allowed to see it if it's a secret?" Natalie asks.

"You're here now," says Ajay. "That makes you part of the team. We don't keep secrets from the team."

Okay. So he's definitely mad I didn't mention the calls with Natalie. He'll just have to get over it.

Zoey grabs a fat folder off a nearby workbench and begins to pull out sketches and plans for our Trojan unicorn. One by one, she hands them to Natalie, who examines each drawing carefully. "This is amazing," Natalie says.

Zoey actually blushes. "We made it so that you can come to the parade with us."

Ajay shows Natalie the tall wooden frame we've already assembled. "We'll attach the cardboard body to the frame, then bolt everything to a plywood base that rolls. You can ride on the inside."

"We've still got to figure out how to attach wheels to the platform," I point out.

"Only if you want it to roll," says Asha.

"Which we do," I say.

"I bet you could modify a metal bracket for the wheel mount," Natalie suggests. "It should probably go on a piece of two-by-four, and you'll need a couple lock washers and a hex nut to keep the axles in place." She makes a quick sketch to help us understand what she means. "That setup won't last forever, but it should be good enough for a day or two."

Ajay studies the drawing. "That's a really good idea," he says.

"I like making things," Natalie tells us. "I want to be an engineer one day. My hero is Hedy Lamarr."

"Who's Hedy Lamarr?" asks Ajay.

"She was one of the biggest names from the Golden Age of Hollywood," offers Zoey. "She was a leading lady with Jimmy Stewart and Clark Gable and pretty much anybody who was anybody. Some people say she was the most beautiful woman in the world. She was the inspiration for Cat Woman and for Walt Disney's Snow White. She played Delilah in *Samson and Delilah*, but my favorite Hedy Lamarr movie is—"

"*Her Highness and the Bellboy*?" says Natalie.

"How did you know?" asks Zoey.

Natalie smiles. "Danny told me you like romantic comedies. I love the part where Hedy Lamarr learns she's going to be queen, and the bellboy thinks he's going to be king."

"You've really seen it!" says Zoey.

"What does this have to do with engineering?" asks Ajay.

"Hedy Lamarr was also an amazing inventor and a self-taught engineer," Natalie tells him. "I did a report about her for school. At the same time she was starring in the movies, she made breakthroughs in aerodynamics, she played around with chemistry, she even created a better stoplight. But her most important work was in communications systems. Her inventions paved the way for Wi-Fi, GPS, and bunch of other technology we use in cell phones now. I hope I can be a little bit like her."

Zoey points at Natalie's sketch for the wheel mount. "You're on the right track."

"For engineering and for beauty," says Asha.

Now it's Natalie's turn to blush.

"Don't be embarrassed," says Zoey. "We were all thinking it."

Asha grabs a pair of safety glasses and lowers them over her face. "Ladies, it's time to make stuff."

Ajay crosses his arms across his chest. "I am no lady."

Asha laughs at her brother. "I agree. And we should probably keep Danny away from pointy things for a while too."

Ajay and I head inside to get snacks for everybody. I'm surprised to find no one sitting in the kitchen, but voices come from the living room down the hall. I peek around the corner and see that Mrs. Kalli is serving plates of fruit, cupcakes, and a kind of banana fritter that is so delicious that I'm tempted to barge in and steal one for myself. I return to the kitchen and corner Ajay, who is standing on a step stool and pulling snack foods out of a closet. "Your mother made pazham pori!" I tell him.

"She won't let us near them," he warns me.

"I thought she was just going to make tea."

Ajay laughs. "Have you met my mother?"

I glance at a plaque covered in Sanskrit script hanging above the kitchen sink. I can't actually read it, but Mrs. Kalli let me know that it is a phrase common in India. It means *The guest is equivalent to God*. In other words, hospitality is a big deal in this house.

Ajay piles pretzels, potato chips, and a package of cookies into my arms. I grab a huge bag of red licorice too.

Back in the garage, we find Zoey mixing paint. Asha is drilling a hole through a piece of metal, and Natalie's slicing up cardboard with the utility knife. "Be careful with that," I tell her.

Natalie lowers the knife. "Check this out." She attaches a jewel-shaped cutout to a long strip of cardboard that's rolled and taped into a crown-sized circle. She staples a pair of intricate cardboard wings on either side of a crown that now looks like an amazing battle helmet. She lowers the whole thing over her head. "What do you think?"

"That's awesome!" I say. And it really is.

"It's more Norse god than Trojan War," Natalie says a little apologetically.

"Don't worry," Zoey tells her. "Unicorns love Valkyries."

"This is what it will look like when it's done." Natalie takes out her phone and shows us a picture of a winged headpiece that looks like it's constructed out of silver, bronze, and leather.

Asha leans forward. "You can make that?"

"I spend a lot of time with the prop people when I'm on set. You'd be surprised at how much you can do with duct tape, cardboard, and spray paint." She removes the winged helmet and places it on Asha's head. "This one's for you."

Asha puts a hand to the cardboard wings on her head. "But—"

"I'm going to make a Spartan helmet that covers my whole face," Natalie tells her. "That way I can pull the unicorn without anybody recognizing me."

"You don't have to worry about that," Ajay reminds her. "You're going to be on the inside."

Natalie places both hands on her hips, tilts her head back, and replies with a voice that could fill an auditorium. "In time the savage bull doth bear the yoke."

Apparently, Natalie intends to pull the unicorn.

"Helmet or not," I tell her. "People will know who you are if you go around quoting lines from *Mutant Zombie Soul Pirates* all day."

Natalie laughs. "Danny, that's Shakespeare."

"Natalie," says Ajay. "*Mutant Zombie Soul Pirates* was good, but it wasn't that good."

Chapter 13

you can never have too many battle helmets

By the time Gram and our moms are done chatting in Mrs. Kalli's living room, Natalie and I have assembled several cardboard battle helmets. "You can never have too many battle helmets," she tells me.

Meanwhile, Asha and Ajay have created four new wheel mounts thanks to Natalie's directions and a bag of old metal brackets we found at the bottom of a toolbox. Also, Zoey's mostly finished cutting out the unicorn, which, when assembled, will be the size of a small school bus. Perhaps just as importantly, there have been no additional injuries.

"Natalie," says Mrs. Griffin when she returns to the garage, "let's head to your aunt's house and wash up. We're having dinner tonight with Danny and his mother."

I remember that Gram is hosting her garden club this evening. I'm not sure if her absence will be a good thing or a bad thing.

"I hope everybody likes Italian," Mom announces. "When your name is Constantino, everything is Italian."

"I bet there's no spinach smoothies in Naples," Gram mutters.

Probably it's a good thing that Gram's not joining us.

Natalie removes the safety glasses still covering her face. "Thanks for letting me help," she says to all of us.

Asha gives her a big smile. "You should come back tomorrow."

"I'd like that."

"So would we," says Zoey.

Ajay puts his hands on his hips. "I was going to say that."

Natalie glances at Mrs. Griffin, who gives a nod. "Great," Natalie says. "See you tomorrow."

She's barely gone when Asha starts jumping up and down like a third grader who just learned she's getting a pony. "This is happening! This is really happening!"

"This is happening to Danny," Ajay points out. "Not to you."

Asha ignores her brother. "One day, when Natalie and Danny are married and they have five or seven kids, we will visit their big house in California, and we'll look back and know that it all started today!"

"Whoa!" I say. "What's with the five or seven kids?"

"Didn't it really start a few days ago when you stole Danny's phone?" Ajay asks his sister.

Zoey turns to me. "Does Natalie know that Asha sort of orchestrated this whole thing?"

"Not exactly," I say.

Zoey stares at me without speaking.

"Not at all," I clarify.

"When are you going to tell her?"

"Why does he have to tell her?" says Asha.

"Remember what I told you about rom-com complications?" asks Zoey.

"This is not a complication," I say.

"It's definitely comedy," says Ajay.

"It might be romance," offers Asha.

Ajay laughs at me. "I hope there's some romance if five or seven children are in your future."

"Danny," says Zoey, "lies are always complications."

I pick up one of the cardboard helmets that Natalie and I made together. "I haven't lied to anybody."

Once again, Zoey replies with silence.

"The only people that know the real story are you, me, Asha, and Ajay," I add.

"That's all?" says Zoey.

"And my grandmother."

"And your mom," adds Asha.

"Are you the one that told her?" I ask.

Asha shrugs. "I didn't know it was a secret."

Zoey counts everybody out on her fingers. "That's

just enough for a volleyball team but too many to keep a secret."

"Zoey's right," Ajay tells me. "Just let Natalie know how it happened."

I study the cardboard helmet in my hands. Natalie showed me how to use duct tape and metallic spray paint to make the thing look fantastic. So far, the whole day's been kind of fantastic. Why risk ruining it with information that's not important?

"I'll think about it," I say.

"You're about to make a classic mistake," Zoey tells me. "You think this is a story that's just about you. But Natalie wants something too. Actually, I think it's even more than that. She didn't come all the way to Cuper Cove just for the fun of it. That girl needs something, Danny."

I look up and study the giant unicorn staring down at me from her spot against the wall. "What could Natalie Flores Griffin possibly need?"

"I have no idea," says Zoey, "but keeping secrets is not going to help you find out."

A couple hours later, I step into the kitchen just in time to see a tall pot of boiling water bubble and spill onto our stovetop. While I turn off the burner, Mom opens and closes the oven door like a giant fan. She's trying to clear a cloud of black smoke coming from two garlic bread loaves that are still on fire. Before I can speak, the smoke alarm on the ceiling starts to squeal. It appears that my perfect day is over.

"What are you doing?" I ask my mother. I try—and fail—to keep the panic out of my voice.

"I'm cooking," Mom snaps.

"You can't cook!" I remind her.

"You might have mentioned that before I planned a dinner party."

"I thought you knew."

Mom closes the oven door, grabs a broom, and uses the handle to stab the smoke alarm, which finally snaps off the ceiling and falls to the floor. Unfortunately, the alarm continues to sound. "Would you please?" Mom yells at me.

"Please what?"

She points at the screaming alarm. "Help me deal with this!"

I grab the remains of the alarm and yank out the battery. At the same time, Mom pulls a small red extinguisher from beneath the sink and blasts it into the oven. Once the fire is out, she removes the smoking bread and tosses it into the pot on the stove.

"What do you think about bread soup?" says Mom.

"What do you think about eating out?" I say.

Mom hands me the broom. "You clean up. I'm going to make a couple calls."

By the time Natalie and Mrs. Griffin arrive, Mom's wearing a fresh floral-print dress, the kitchen is clean, and I'm covered in dish soap, fire extinguisher chemicals, and scouring powder. "Change of plans," Mom announces when we gather in the living room. "We're meeting everybody in town."

"Everybody?" Natalie, Mrs. Griffin, and I all say at the same time.

"I've phoned ahead," Mom says. "My friend Benny has a table for us. I promise you'll love it."

Benny's is a fancy seafood restaurant where we go when Mom sells an especially big house, but I'm still wearing jeans, a T-shirt, and an apron that says KISS ME! I'M ITALIAN! Not only that, I smell like charcoal, garlic, and lemon-scented bleach. "I can't go to Benny's like this."

Mom shoots me a strained smile. "Then hurry up and change."

I turn and head straight to the upstairs bathroom, where I toss the apron and dirty clothes into the tub and then clean up as best as possible. It doesn't make sense to put smelly clothes back on, so I wrap myself in a towel and make a dash for my bedroom. Unfortunately, I find Natalie just inside my bedroom door.

"Don't turn around!" I say.

Natalie turns around. When she sees that I'm wearing almost nothing, she quickly spins away and continues to examine the comic book pages and hand-drawn artwork on my walls. "I am going to pretend that you're just getting back from a swimming pool, and you're wearing a bathing suit beneath that towel," she tells me.

"Great," I say. "Because I am going to pretend that this isn't happening at all."

She laughs, then nods toward some of the heroes and villains and monsters pasted all over my room. "Do you like comics?"

"What makes you think that?"

Natalie points at the picture of a giant green creature at eye level. "That's Fin Fang Foom, giant alien dragon from the planet Kakaranathara who sleeps in a secret cave somewhere deep beneath the surface of China."

"You know Fin Fang Foom?"

"I was supposed to get a part in *Mandarin Dragon: The Fin Fang Foom Story,* but then the movie never happened."

"Because it's kind of racist?" I ask.

She nods. "I think that had something to do with it."

"What was your part?" I ask.

"Girl that gets eaten by Fin Fang Foom." Natalie taps a finger on a picture of Wonder Woman. "I was up for this movie too, but then they cast someone else."

I point at my sketch of the Incredible Hulk. "Hulk smash movie people!"

Natalie smiles, then stands on tiptoe to get a better look at a Superman drawing I've tacked just below the ceiling. "Did you make that? It's really good." She leans forward and reads the Superman quote I've jotted above the Man of Steel's head. "*There is a superhero in all of us, we just need the courage to put on the cape.*" She pauses. "I bet you wish you had a cape right now."

"I am a little chilly," I admit.

"I came upstairs to use the bathroom," she tells me.

"It's across the hall."

The two of us slide around each other without making eye contact. A few minutes later, we're both downstairs again. I'm wearing clean clothes and hoping I no longer smell like a bakery fire. I also hope that Natalie isn't secretly comparing my Popsicle-stick body to the twenty-nine-year-old supermodels and bodybuilders who play teenagers on TV and in the movies.

With Mom hustling us along, we quickly move from living room to driveway to car. Natalie and Mrs. Griffin decide to drive separately, so I volunteer to join them. "I can show them the way," I offer.

"There's only one turn between here and there," Mom tells Mrs. Griffin. "Just follow us. You can't miss it." She grabs my arm and drags me toward her Volvo.

"Or I could come with you," I say to Mom.

"Listen," she says while I buckle my seat belt. "I'm

going to invite Natalie to be our Halloween queen. You better not derail this."

"But—"

"No," Mom says. "I'm not asking you. I'm telling you."

"She's going to say no," I warn my mother.

"We'll see about that."

but that's not all!

A set of Halloween scarecrows dressed like fishermen stand in front of Benny's Restaurant. They wear hip waders, floppy hats, and fishing vests covered in neon lures and feathered flies. One holds a pole bent nearly double because it's hooked something that looks like a great white shark made out of hay bales.

"Excuse me," says Natalie. She points at a huge plastic lobster mounted above the restaurant's front door. "Is this a seafood restaurant?"

"Benny's is the best," Mom promises. "Whatever you order tonight was swimming in the Atlantic this morning."

"My mother is allergic to seafood," Natalie tells us.

Mom dismisses this with a wave. "Not to worry. They have plenty of other things on the menu."

"It's not a problem," Mrs. Griffin adds. "I know how to be careful."

Natalie and I exchange a quick look. Our mothers are determined to be invincible even if it kills them.

We step inside the restaurant, where Mom appears to know just about everybody. A waitress leads us to the center of the room. A long table is already half-filled with people familiar to me as well. Maddie's parents, Mr. and Mrs. MacSweeney, are at one end. Billy Bennet's dad, who looks like a supersized version of Billy, sits near Mr. Maggio from school. I recognize Mr. Gilbert Wall, a tall, elderly man who sits on Cuper Cove's city council. And that's when I realize that all these people are on the Cuper Cove Halloween festival committee. Some of them are Missy for Mayor volunteers too.

"What's going on?" I whisper to my mother.

"I told you," she says. "I made some calls."

Before I can say anything else, she raises both hands in the air. The signal brings every person in the restaurant to their feet. The whole place turns to Natalie and starts to cheer.

"Welcome!" Mom says into a wireless microphone that's somehow appeared in her hand. "Please join me in welcoming Natalie Flores Griffin home to Cuper Cove!"

The applause grows louder while Natalie and Mrs. Flores Griffin, who both look kind of stunned, make their way to their seats. Natalie takes the chair next to mine. She smiles, waves at the crowd, and whispers to me through gritted teeth, "Did you know anything about this?"

"No," I promise.

"Are there going to be any more surprises?"

Before I can reply, Mom raises her hands and uses the microphone once again. "But wait," she says. "There's more!"

"There might be more," I warn Natalie.

"If you serve on my campaign committee," Mom says into the mic, "you know that we'd planned to meet later this evening for dessert."

Natalie shoots me a look.

I shake my head. "I have no idea what she's talking about."

"But then I set my kitchen on fire," Mom explains.

The crowd laughs. They think she's kidding. Suddenly I wonder if the fire was an accident.

"I swear it was just an accident," Mom says as if she can read my mind. "Either way, thank you for coming out a little earlier than planned. Our host, Benny Sergiyenko and his daughter, Mira, have prepared a very special Halloween treat, but instead of making that treat just for us, I've asked Benny to make a few changes so we can take this opportunity to honor our favorite Hollywood movie star and our hometown hero, Natalie Flores Griffin."

Now everybody is clapping again. "Benny," Mom shouts above the applause. "Show us what you've got!"

Suddenly, the lights go dim. Two double doors leading from the kitchen pop open, and Mr. Sergiyenko pushes a rolling cart into the restaurant. On the cart, a giant three-tiered Halloween cake features pumpkin-orange icing, chocolate-drizzle spiderwebs, and candy-corn highlights. Not only that, flaming sparklers stick out of the top of the cake and illuminate the room in a flickering glow. Even without a signal from Mom, the crowd bursts into another round of applause. At the same time Mira, wearing a black cape across her shoulders and a pointy witch's hat on her head, follows the Halloween cake into the room.

"That's the little redheaded girl that I told you about," I whisper to Natalie.

"The one who's praying for me?"

I nod. "That's the one."

"You didn't tell me she was a witch."

"I'm having a hard time keeping up with it all."

Mira's dad, a thick-necked, bald-headed man, brings the cake to our end of the table. He gives a nod to Mom, Natalie, and Mrs. Griffin, then turns to his daughter. "Mira, you're up."

The room goes silent as Mira steps around the cake and approaches Natalie. Mira's hands are shaking, and her voice quivers when she speaks. "H-h-hi, Natalie."

Natalie stands to greet the girl. "Hello, Mira," she says kindly. "Danny's told me all about you."

Mira's eyes go wide. "He has?"

Natalie nods. "Thank you for the cake."

"But that's not all," Mira says softly.

"Oh?" Natalie moves her foot slightly so that it's on top of mine. Slowly but surely, she starts to increase her weight on my toes.

Mira leans forward. "Would you—"

Mom shoves the microphone closer to Mira's face. "You'll have to speak up, honey."

Mira nods and starts again. "Natalie Flores Griffin, will you be our Cuper Cove Halloween queen this year?"

Suddenly, my foot feels like an elephant's standing on it, which I suppose is only fair since Natalie must be feeling the exact same weight right now.

"I . . ." Natalie pauses, then reaches for the microphone that's still in my mother's hand.

Mom moves the mic away. "Congratulations!" she hollers to the crowd. "To all of us!"

Again, the room fills with applause while waiters and waitresses rush appetizer plates onto every table.

"Thank you!" Mira says to Natalie over the din.

Natalie offers a painful grin. "My pleasure."

"I'm sorry," I whisper to Natalie.

"I'm going to kill you," she replies.

"This is not my fault!" I protest.

"I don't care," says Natalie. "Somebody has to die, and it might as well be you."

"Before you kill Danny," says Mrs. Griffin, who's been following the exchange between her daughter and me, "I have a question."

"What?" Natalie and I say at the same time.

Mrs. Griffin licks her lips, then points at a plate on the table in front of us. "Are those fried onion rings?"

I shake my head. "That's calamari."

"Uh-oh," says Mrs. Griffin.

"What's calamari?" Natalie asks.

"Fried squid," I tell her.

Quickly, Natalie turns, grabs her mother's purse, and dumps the whole thing into my lap. Out of the pile of keys, hairbrushes, credit cards, and Post-it notes, she grabs a plastic tube labeled EPI-PEN.

"What's happening?" I say.

"Maybe nothing," says Natalie. "Or maybe anaphylactic shock."

"I think it might be a mild case of the second thing," says Mrs. Griffin, whose face is turning bright red.

"What's that?" I ask.

"She's having an allergic reaction to the squid." Natalie reaches beneath the table, hikes up her mother's skirt, and stabs the pen into Mrs. Griffin's thigh. Somehow, she manages to do all this so calmly and smoothly that nobody even notices. "Whose dumb idea was it to turn squid into food?" Natalie asks in an angry whisper.

"It's very good," I tell her. "You should try it."

"It is surprisingly tasty," Mrs. Griffin agrees a little breathlessly.

Natalie closes her eyes. "I am not eating a squid."

I glance at Mrs. Griffin. "Are you going to be okay?"

She nods. "I'll be fine, but we should probably go."

Natalie glances at my lap. "Put that stuff back into my mom's purse."

I move everything back into the bag as Natalie stands up.

"Excuse me!" she says. Even without the microphone, Natalie's voice fills the room, and the buzz of laughter and conversation dies down immediately. "Thank you." She pauses and scans the room like a general preparing to address her troops. "Thank you," she says again. "Thank you so much for this lovely get-together. This is all so unexpected. I am very surprised and incredibly honored that I can be this year's Cuper Cove Halloween festival queen. I still think of Cuper Cove as my true home."

Mom starts to clap, but Natalie holds up a hand and puts a stop to that.

"Of course," Natalie continues, "we do live in California now. My mom and I only got back to Cuper Cove this morning. It's been a very long day, and I'm afraid that the travel and the jet lag are catching up with both of us. I hope you'll forgive us for stepping out a little early, but I look forward to seeing you all again soon."

This time, she accepts a polite round of applause before

leaning over and whispering into my ear, "Help me get my mother to the car."

I stand and offer Mrs. Griffin my arm. "Were you telling the truth just now?" I say to Natalie. "Are you really honored to be Cuper Cove's Halloween queen?"

"Danny," says Natalie, "that's called acting."

"You're very good," I say.

"Shut up," Natalie tells me.

We make our way to the parking lot, where the fresh air seems to be helping Mrs. Griffin clear her head. "Can you drive?" I ask her.

She nods. "I'm feeling much better. Plus I grew up in Cuper Cove. I could find my way around here with my eyes closed."

I forgot that Cuper Cove is Mrs. Griffin's hometown too. "Did you go to school with my mother?" I ask.

Mrs. Griffin shakes her head. "She's a little older than me. We moved in different circles back then. Until you and Natalie were in school together, Missy and I never talked. I never knew your dad. He passed away before you were in preschool, plus he didn't grow up around here." Mrs. Griffin is nervous and sort of babbling, which is probably not unusual after you're nearly killed by a piece of squid. "I remember your mom used to date a boy named Shad. I always thought that was a wonderful name. And now I'm allergic to fish. Isn't that funny?"

"Shad?" I say. "Shad Beamon?"

Before Mrs. Griffin can reply, Mira races out of the restaurant with a small box in her hands. "Natalie!" she cries. "Your cake! Take a piece of cake!"

Natalie closes her eyes, gathers herself with a deep breath, then offers Mira a big smile. "Can I make a different suggestion?" she asks.

"What is it?" says Mira.

"You keep the cake for now. If you don't mind, I'll come back tomorrow so that we can share some together."

"Just you and me?" says Mira.

Natalie nods. "Just you and me."

Mira smiles and then, without warning, she gives Natalie a quick hug. "See you tomorrow!"

Mira races back to the restaurant while Natalie heads to the car that her mom's already started.

"I thought you were coming to Ajay's tomorrow," I remind her.

"I want to do that," Natalie says as she climbs into the passenger seat. "I hope I can do that. But doing everything that I want to do is rarely an option for me anymore."

"I know what you mean," I say.

"Danny," she says. "I don't think you do."

Chapter 15

i used to be a kid with a dog

Sunday starts gray and overcast, but a breeze from the ocean, which is only a few miles away, blows in and sweeps the sky clean. By mid-afternoon, everything glows blue and bright. It's good that the wind is low and the sun shining, because we've got a team assembling Cooper the Trojan Unicorn in front of Ajay's house right now. Billy and Maddie are working with Asha to organize pieces of Cooper's cardboard body in the driveway. Zoey holds a long tape measure for Darius, who is calculating the proper length for a unicorn neck. Ajay and I find a couple big eye bolts to screw onto the front of our rolling platform. "When will Natalie be here?" asks Billy.

"Is that the only reason you're helping?" I ask.

"Yes," says Billy.

"No," says Darius.

"Maybe," says Maddie.

After last night, I don't expect that Natalie will be joining us today.

"Don't hold your breath," I tell my friends.

I turn back to the eye bolts. Once they're secure, we'll attach a long length of rope to tow our Trojan unicorn in the pep rally and parade.

"You really think Natalie isn't coming?" Asha asks me.

I shake my head. "I don't want to talk about it."

Of course, Asha doesn't need me to talk about it because the whole town already knows everything about everything. Since last night, Mom added a special announcement to the official Halloween festival website as well as to her own Missy for Mayor pages. According to the news release, Missy Constantino recruited Natalie Flores Griffin to serve as this year's surprise celebrity Halloween queen. There's even a photograph of Mom with Natalie, Mira, and Benny's amazing pumpkin cake, which I have to admit is the most remarkable baked good I've ever seen.

"I think Natalie will be here," says Ajay, who is kneeling on the ground beside me.

"How do you know?" I ask.

"She's at the end of the driveway right now."

I look up, and sure enough Natalie's hopping off an old fat-tired bike. She leans the bicycle against a tree and then pulls a small white box from a wire basket attached to the handlebars.

Ajay stands to greet her. "What did you bring us?" he asks.

"Do you like cake?" Natalie asks him.

"Did you single-handedly save the prince of the universe and defeat an entire space fleet of mutant zombie soul pirates with nothing but courage, spunk, and charm?"

Natalie comes closer. "You realize that was a cartoon, right?"

Ajay nods. "You realize I don't care, right?"

Natalie walks up to me and pushes the cake box into my hands. "Hold this," she says. "I have to text my mom." She pulls her phone from a fanny pack and then punches out a quick message. "Letting me take a bike and ride around town by myself is not something either one of us is used to."

"Is that your aunt's bike?" I ask.

Natalie nods. "Pretty cool, huh?"

Honestly, the bike looks like something you might find washed up on the beach at low tide. "How far did you ride?"

"My aunt's house is just a couple miles away, but first I went back to the restaurant."

"Did you eat cake with Mira?" I ask.

"I definitely ate cake with Mira," says Natalie. "It was delicious. That's why I'm going to eat more cake with you." She puts her phone away and then points behind me. "Is that Darius Bryan, Billy Bennet, and Madeline MacSweeney?"

I turn and find Billy, Maddie, and Darius staring at Natalie with big dumb grins. "I didn't think you'd remember us," says Billy.

Natalie gives him a smile. "I remember pinning you in under twenty seconds at the Cuper Cove Pee Wee Pirate Wrestling tournament."

"I lasted thirty-five," says Darius.

"What about you?" I ask Madeline.

Billy puts an arm around Maddie's shoulder. "Maddie was Cuper Cove Pee Wee Pirate Wrestling champ!"

"Only because Natalie got disqualified," Maddie tells us.

"For crushing people?" I guess.

Natalie shrugs. "Apparently that's not a legal move."

Zoey steps up, takes the cake box out of my hands, and then turns to Natalie. "Danny was just saying that he wanted to take you for a walk today."

I turn to Zoey. "Wha—"

"Where are we going?" Natalie asks me.

"I—"

Zoey interrupts me. "Anywhere is fine. You can walk around the block and see everybody's Halloween decorations while you talk."

"That sounds nice," says Natalie.

"But you can leave the cake," says Billy.

Zoey holds up the box. "I've got it."

Natalie turns to me. "Lead the way."

Zoey actually gives us a little shove so that a moment later, Natalie and I are turning around the corner and heading into my neighborhood. A few houses have pumpkins and simple sidewalk scarecrows, but there's nothing fancy. It's not that kind of neighborhood.

"How's your mom?" I ask.

"She's okay," says Natalie. "The medicine took care of it."

We walk a few more steps without speaking. "Do you want to crush me?" I finally ask.

Before she can reply, I stub my toe and trip over a piece of sidewalk slab that's been heaved out of place by frost. "Maybe I should hold your hand instead," Natalie suggests.

"No," I say. "That's okay."

"Oh." She sounds disappointed, and I realize that I just screwed something up, so—by accident on purpose—I trip again. This time, I reach out and grab Natalie's hand. She wraps her fingers in mine and helps me regain my balance.

I can't remember the last time I held anybody's hand. It feels surprisingly good. Plus, it's nice to know that Natalie doesn't want me to fall on my face.

"You have big hands," I say.

Suddenly I suspect I might have said another stupid

thing, but apparently not, because Natalie laughs. "I can almost palm a basketball," she tells me.

"Do you play basketball?"

"Just with my dad. He has a hoop in his driveway."

"I'm kind of terrible at anything that involves a ball," I admit.

"Me too," says Natalie. "I just like hanging out with my dad."

I never actually spoke with Natalie's father when we were younger. "He used to carry you on his back," I remember. "And he had a beard."

"I don't get piggyback rides anymore," Natalie says, "but he still has a beard. You would like him. He's a painter."

"Like a house painter or like a *Mona Lisa* painter?"

"Both. That's why we left Cuper Cove. My father is an artist. He thought there would be more opportunities for his work in California. And there are. But he still paints a lot of houses too."

A quick breeze sweeps autumn leaves across our feet, and the October chill makes us both shiver. I wonder what it's like in California right now. "I thought you moved because you got discovered in Hollywood."

Natalie shakes her head. "That's just a publicity story my mother made up. I got discovered because I went on a thousand different auditions."

"Plus you're really talented," I say. "And you're movie star pretty too."

"Almost everybody in the movie business is talented," Natalie tells me. "And makeup artists turn supermodels into monsters and monsters into supermodels every day."

"Are you wearing makeup right now?" I ask.

Natalie gives me a funny look. "No. Why?"

"You don't look like a monster."

She gives me a smile. "Thanks."

I point at a FOR SALE sign in front of a small pink house across the street. "If you lived in Cuper Cove, we could be neighbors."

"I would love to live in Cuper Cove."

"Really?" I ask.

We continue walking while Natalie talks. "The main job of kid actors is to be on time, don't fidget, and cry on cue. I think I'm ready to do more. Or maybe less. I'm not sure."

"Why don't you quit?"

"My mom works really hard so I can be—"

"NATALIE FLORES GRIFFIN?" I say in a fake movie announcer voice.

Natalie grins. "Don't get me wrong. I like being NATALIE FLORES GRIFFIN. But I think just Natalie would be okay too."

"My mother wants me to be a U.S. Marine like my dad," I share as we continue around the block.

"But that's not what you want?" Natalie asks.

"Honestly," I say, "I don't know what I want."

"I bet you want other people to stop telling you what you want so that you can figure it out for yourself."

As a matter of fact, that is exactly what I want.

"How did you know?" I ask.

"Danny," says Natalie, "I think we both want the same thing. I also think you could be a great marine one day if that's what you really want to be."

"That's not what I want to be."

"I didn't think so," says Natalie. "But you never know."

"Thanks," I say. "I think."

We've made our way down the street and around the corner, so we're standing at the end of my own driveway now. I point at the side door leading into my kitchen. "Do you want to come in for something to drink?"

"Is anybody home?" Natalie asks.

I don't see my mother's car. "I don't think so."

Natalie shakes her head. "My mom and dad are both pretty strict. They wouldn't want me to visit without adults around."

I feel my cheeks glow red. "I wouldn't—"

"I know," she says. "Those are just their rules."

Somehow, our hands find each other again. We don't have much more to say, but that's all right. We make the final turn that will bring us back to Ajay's house.

"I'm sorry about last night," I say.

"Me too," says Natalie.

"What are you sorry for?"

"I should have said no. I should have told them I wouldn't be the Halloween queen."

"That was a setup," I tell her. "That was my mom."

Natalie shakes her head. "I should have been ready for it. The Halloween festival committee sends me an invitation every year."

"They do?"

"We always lie and say I can't make it," Natalie tells me. "That's not why I want to come to Cuper Cove. I never pass up the chance to be normal for a little while. That's why I went to the parade in disguise last year."

I think again about the *Sidewalk Scarecrows* movie. Again, I decide that it's not important right now. If Natalie has to disguise herself in order to be normal for a little while, then she deserves at least a little privacy.

"That's why my mother didn't want me to go to the dance with you," Natalie continues. "She thought your invitation was just another way to get me to Cuper Cove, but—"

"It wasn't!" I say. "It's not!"

"I didn't think so. I know we'll always be friends."

Natalie gives my hand a squeeze. "We are still friends, right?"

I squeeze back. "Right."

"Good," says Natalie. "Because here's the thing, Danny. I don't think I can go to the dance with you."

I stop. "What? Why not?"

"Look." Natalie points toward Ajay's house where a large group of strangers has gathered at the end of the driveway.

"Who are they?" I ask.

"They're probably fans who tracked me down on the Internet. Once your mom posted her queen of Halloween announcements, it was sort of inevitable."

At the moment, the crowd is oohing and aaahhing over the ten-foot-tall unicorn standing in front of the Kallis' garage. While we watch, a white van labeled ACTION NEWS TV29 pulls up to the curb.

"You don't think they're here for the unicorn?" I ask.

Natalie considers this for a moment. "The unicorn is amazing, but—"

She's interrupted by a yell from the crowd. "There she is!"

Suddenly, the tiny mob turns and starts racing toward us. Behind them, the TV news guy hops out of the van, lifts a camera, and starts to film the action.

"My mother is worried that somebody might get hurt," Natalie tells me.

I watch the people approach. "Do you think they'd believe that Taylor Swift is giving free pumpkin carving lessons in front of City Hall right now?"

"I'm worried too," says Natalie.

"This is a little intimidating," I admit as the crowd gets closer.

"Yup," Natalie agrees.

"Should we run?"

She shakes her head. "That will make it worse. Just don't let go of my hand."

I'm not sure if this is for her safety or my own. "Okay," I promise.

The group moves down the sidewalk, some faster and some slower, until they surround Natalie like water breaking around a boulder. If I weren't holding her hand, I don't think these people would even notice me. Most snap pictures with their phones. A couple have actual cameras. A few scramble for pens and paper. "Can we have your autograph?" they call to Natalie. "Can we get a picture with you?"

Natalie ignores the questions. Instead, she scans the crowd until she finds a small girl who is carrying a stuffed dog. Natalie kneels down so that she can look the girl in the eye. "Hi," she says. "I like your dog."

"Thank you," the girl says matter-of-factly.

"Why do you have a stuffed dog and not a stuffed cat or a bear or something else?" Natalie asks.

The girl nods as if this conversation started several hours ago, and it's about time somebody's finally asking an intelligent question. "I have a stuffed dog because I want to be an animal scientist like Jane Goodall when I grow up, and dogs were Jane Goodall's favorite animals. Also, my parents say I can't have a real dog until I turn eight, and that's two years from now."

"I thought Jane Goodall's favorite animals were gorillas and chimpanzees," says Natalie.

The girl shakes her head. "You're wrong."

Natalie nods. "Thank you for setting me straight."

Somehow, the simple exchange spins this moment into something new. A second ago, the crowd was aggressive and even a little scary. Now there's a sense of fun and even joy thanks to Natalie's gentle kindness.

The low rumble of a big muscle car engine comes from behind the crowd, which has spilled into the street. I know that sound. "I think your ride is here," I tell Natalie.

"My ride?" she asks.

"My grandmother's coming to the rescue," I whisper.

Natalie turns to the crowd. "Thank you for coming out to say hello." She offers them all a quick wave. "Have a nice afternoon, everybody."

Still holding my hand, she steps into the group that's standing between us and the street. Fortunately, everyone makes way as we move forward. We reach the center of the road, where, just as I expected, Gram waits behind the wheel of the green Camaro. Natalie slides into the passenger seat, closes the door, and rolls down her window.

"How did you do that?" I ask through the window. "How did you get the whole crowd on your side?"

"When in doubt," she tells me, "find a kid with a dog."

"I used to be a kid with a dog."

Natalie smiles. "That doesn't surprise me, Danny."

I offer a little wave as Gram drops the Camaro into gear and drives away.

Chapter 13

this is not a dark night of the soul

Ajay finds me at the bus stop in the morning. "Where did you go yesterday?" he asks. "We put everything together without you, and then we had to put it all away too. We could have used some help."

"I'm sorry," I tell him. "I just went home."

"Billy, Darius, and Madeline are coming back after school today," he continues. "They're going to help us finish so everything can be ready for the pep rally on Thursday, then the parade on Friday."

"I don't know if I'm going to make it," I tell him.

"What do you mean?"

"I don't know," I say.

"But—"

"I don't want to talk about it, okay?"

The bus arrives before Ajay can reply. "I know I'm running late," Mr. Beamon tells us as we climb aboard. "But don't worry. This is the school bus that made the Kessel run in less than twelve parsecs."

Sometimes, even Star Wars fans can find other Star Wars fans annoying.

Zoey joins us a few minutes later. "Where did you go yesterday?" she asks me.

"He doesn't want to talk about it," Ajay tells her.

"Natalie's not going to the dance with me," I blurt out. "Okay?"

"Whoa," says Zoey. "It's a little early for a dark night of the soul."

"It's just a stupid dance," I say. "I didn't want to go in the first place."

"Then why are you upset?" she asks.

"Because now I want to go."

"And Natalie doesn't?"

I shrug. "I don't know."

"What did you do?" says Ajay.

I look outside just in time to see a sidewalk scarecrow holding a MISSY FOR MAYOR sign. "It's not my fault," I tell my friends.

"Is it Natalie's fault?" asks Ajay.

The bus goes over a big bump, which causes my backpack to bounce off my lap and onto the floor. "Are you aiming for the potholes?" I shout at Mr. Beamon.

The bus driver shoots an annoyed look at me through his rearview mirror.

"It might not be anybody's fault," offers Zoey. "On

the other hand, blame is an important ingredient in most romantic comedies."

I shake my head. "Natalie's not the problem. It's the whole world that's the problem."

"Classic rom-com," Zoey says thoughtfully.

"This is not a rom-com!" I yell at her.

"She didn't say it was," Ajay snaps at me.

We ride the rest of the way without speaking. When we get to school, Ajay and Zoey grab their stuff and head off the bus without me.

"Danny," Mr. Beamon says before I leave. "Wait just a minute."

I step aside and let everyone move past. Finally, I'm the last student remaining. Mr. Beamon closes the school bus door. "Is everything okay?"

"I don't know," I admit.

"Yelling at your friends probably isn't going to help."

I shift the backpack on my shoulder. "Can I ask you a question?"

Mr. Beamon nods.

"Are you the same Shad that dated my mom in high school?"

He laughs a little. "I am."

"Why are you named after a fish?"

Mr. Beamon smiles. "My dad was a fisherman, and my mom was a history teacher."

I have no idea what that's supposed to mean.

"During the Revolutionary War," he continues, "George Washington's army was near starvation when huge schools of American shad swam up the river near the encampment at Valley Forge. Soldiers who'd eaten nothing but lard and maggot-infested bread for weeks rushed into the water and caught thousands of fish by hand. It was like something out of the Bible. An American miracle. Without shad, most of those soldiers would have had to leave Valley Forge or starve to death. Thanks to the shad, they stayed. Three years later, those men defeated the British at the Battle of Yorktown so that the colonies could become the United States of America. My parents named me after the fish that saved our nation."

"I never read that in any history book," I tell him.

"Because it's probably not true."

"Oh."

"It's the kind of story you make up to prove that God is on your side. After a couple hundred years, everybody just accepts it. But then a few historians visit the Revolutionary War toilet pits at Valley Forge and discover that there aren't any fish bones there."

"That's disappointing," I say.

Mr. Beamon nods. "Toilet pits can be like that. If it makes you feel any better, Shad is also the name of a spunky space pilot from the future who leads a group of ragtag mercenaries to defend his planet against mutant soldiers in the classic sci-fi film *Battle Beyond the Stars*. It's also short for Shadrach, one of three Hebrew boys who got thrown into a furnace by an ancient Babylonian king."

"What happened to them?" I ask.

"Faith, friends, and miracles," Mr. Beamon says simply.

"I could use a miracle."

My bus driver shakes his head. "You don't need a miracle, Danny. You need faith."

"Faith in what?"

"Start with yourself," says Mr. Beamon. "And then go from there."

"Could I have a miracle too?"

"What do you need a miracle for?"

"For my mother," I say. "For my friends. For Natalie Flores Griffin. For everything, I guess."

My bus driver looks suddenly concerned. "What's wrong with your mother?"

"Nothing, but—" I double-check to see that the school bus really is empty, then I lower my voice and tell Mr. Beamon the truth. "I don't want her to win the election."

Mr. Beamon nods thoughtfully. "Danny," he finally says, "your mother is running unopposed. She's the only candidate in the race."

"What?" Perhaps I should have paid closer attention to the campaign from the beginning. "What do you mean?"

"Missy Constantino is going to be the next mayor of Cuper Cove. It's a sure thing. She's the only one that wants the job."

I think about the signs and buttons and pamphlets sitting in piles all over my house. "Then what's all the campaign stuff for?"

"If your mother can get an especially large number of votes," Mr. Beamon explains, "she can assume that most people agree with her agenda and her plans for our town."

"Mr. Beamon," I say, "she's going to assume that most people agree with her no matter how many votes she gets."

Mr. Beamon is still laughing when I step off the bus.

The more I think about Mom's meaningless campaign, the more annoyed I get. In fact, I spend the rest of the morning and most of the afternoon in an angry blur. I skip lunch so I won't have to talk about it with my friends. After school, I sit and stew in the office until Gram brings me home.

"What's bothering you?" Gram asks when I slam her car door.

"I figured something out," I tell her.

She cuts off an old Volkswagen and pulls into traffic. "What did you figure out?"

"I figured out that Mom would rather sell houses

or run for an election she can't lose or be the mayor of Cuper Cove than spend any time with me."

"I see." Gram says nothing else until she brings the green Camaro to a stop in front of my house. She points at Mom's car parked in the driveway. "Maybe you should go inside and tell your mother how you feel."

"I don't want to talk to her right now."

"If you do nothing," Gram tells me, "then probably nothing will change."

"Why am I the one that has to do something?"

"Somebody has to go first." Gram shifts the Camaro into gear, so I step out the car.

"But why me?" I ask.

"Why not you?"

She makes a good point. And I don't care. Once she pulls away, I cut through the neighbors' yards, and I head to Ajay's.

"Look who's here," Ajay says when I get to the garage.

Zoey steps out from behind a nearly fully assembled Trojan unicorn. She's joined by Billy, Maddie, and Darius too. "I told you he'd come," Zoey says to everybody.

"I'm sorry," I say. "It's just—"

"You don't have to explain yourself," Zoey tells me. "It's not unusual to be grouchy after a dark night of the soul."

"I am not having a dark night of the soul," I insist.

"In that case," says Zoey, "you really do owe us an apology."

"I'm sorry," I say again. "I'll try to be better."

Zoey puts her hands on her hips. *"Try not. Do. Or do not. There is no try."*

But seriously, Star Wars fans can be very, very annoying.

I point at the unicorn pieces all around us. The giant head sits on the garage floor. The body—a big cardboard box with legs painted on its sides—is mounted on the rolling platform. At the back, a long tail made from several pieces of clothesline rope serves as a handle for the hatchway that leads inside the Trojan unicorn.

"How are we going to get all this to the parade?" I ask.

"My dad's got a delivery truck," says Zoey. "He'll come after school tomorrow to load everything for the pep rally." She grabs a thick black marker. "Now's the time for finishing touches."

I find a hammer and a tin can filled with small nails. Working with Madeline and Billy, I secure stray flaps of cardboard to the pine frame that is now our unicorn's skeleton. At the same time, Ajay and Asha finish the rolling platform while Darius and Zoey use paints and markers to highlight hooves and hocks and a bold, horsey face.

"Danny," says Maddie, "is Natalie Flores Griffin really coming to the pep rally?"

"I'm not sure," I tell her.

Zoey stops detailing the unicorn. "What do you mean you're not sure?"

I bang a nail through a piece of cardboard and into the wooden frame. "We didn't make any final plans."

"Don't you think you should do that?" says Ajay.

Ajay is right. I should call Natalie about the pep rally. And while I'm at it, I should tell her how her whole visit sort of happened because of Asha. I should tell her that I might have made kindness and peace seem possible for her, but she made losing a best friend seem possible for me. And now it feels like I am learning that lesson all over again.

I step back to get a better view of the Trojan unicorn. Thanks to Zoey, Cooper's got a thick, curly mane now. Also, Darius has braided Cooper's tail into something that looks like a cross between a macramé planter and a nest of snakes.

"Danny," says Zoey, "are you going to call Natalie or not?"

"You know what?" I say. "One of you should call her yourself."

Chapter 17

i don't know if those are her real teeth

On Wednesday morning, Mr. Maggio finds me at my locker. "Mr. Constantino," the principal asks, "are you and Natalie ready for tomorrow's pep rally?"

"As ready as we're going to be," I tell him.

For the rest of the day, I do my best to avoid all human contact because who the heck knows what else I might have to lie about. Still, people shout at me in the hallway and corner me in classrooms.

WAS THAT YOU ON TV WITH NATALIE FLORES GRIFFIN?

Yes.

WHEN ARE WE GOING TO MEET HER?

I don't know.

WHAT IS NATALIE REALLY LIKE?

That's a good question.

My friends find me at my locker before lunch. "Where have you been all day?" asks Madeline.

"Danny," says Billy, "are you coming to the cafeteria?"

I shake my head. "I—"

Darius interrupts before I can finish. "Danny's a celebrity now. He doesn't sit with the little people."

"You're six feet tall," Maddie reminds Darius.

"So?" he says.

"It's not just the little people Danny doesn't sit with."

"You guys," I say. "I just don't want to deal with—"

"Go," says Maddie. "Go eat your avocado roll and your sushi toast with your Hollywood girlfriend."

"For your information," I say, "my lunch for the last week has been nothing but dried-out packages of peanut butter crackers while I hide in the school office."

Billy holds up a greasy paper bag. "Sit next to me, and you can have some of my pizza."

"You brought a pizza in a paper bag?" says Darius.

Maddie retrieves a plastic lunch box from her own locker. "He doesn't mean the whole pizza."

"Yes, I do," says Billy.

"Thank you," I tell Billy, "but I'm going to eat with my grandmother today. I am not enjoying being the center of attention all the time."

Darius shrugs. "It must be tough to be as popular as you, Danny."

"That's not what I mean."

My friends slam their lockers and turn away.

By the end of the school day, I'm walking around with a sweatshirt hood over my head. I'm trying to make it to the office without getting trapped by more questions about Natalie. Every time I think I've heard them all, somebody pops up with a new one. WHAT'S NATALIE'S FAVORITE HALLOWEEN CANDY? WHAT DOES SHE THINK ABOUT HARRY POTTER? DOES SHE LIKE PINEAPPLE ON HER PIZZA? ARE ZOMBIE SOUL PIRATES SMARTER THAN THE GHOST PIRATES OF VOOJU ISLAND? ARE THOSE HER REAL TEETH?

Why do people care about these things? Why do they think I know them?

I keep moving, and I almost make it too, but tiny Mira Sergiyenko steps between me and the office door at the last minute. "Danny!" she says. "I'm glad I caught you!"

"I don't know if they're her real teeth, okay?"

"Huh?" says Mira.

"They look real to me," I tell her.

Mira tilts her head a little. "Are you okay?"

"What if I am? What if I'm not? It's not like anybody cares."

"I care," says Mira.

I take a deep breath, then let it out slowly. "Thank you," I say. "I appreciate that."

Mira pushes red hair out of her face, reaches into her backpack, and pulls out a fat envelope that's clearly stuffed with cash. She pushes it toward me. "And could you give this to Natalie?"

"Mira," I say. "I am not a mailman. Also, I don't think Natalie needs any money."

I have no idea whether Natalie needs money or not, but I am very certain that I'm no mailman.

It doesn't matter because Mira continues as if I haven't said a word. "My dad added Natalie's Halloween cake to our dessert menu. We're donating all proceeds from cake sales to the Natalie Flores Griffin Foundation. Rather than put the money in the mail, I thought it would be easier if you just gave it to her."

"What exactly is the Natalie Flores Griffin Foundation?" I ask.

"The Natalie Flores Griffin Foundation raises money to promote healthy food choices in school cafeterias across the nation," Mira explains. "Her mission is 'Let's Eat Something Good Today!'"

"And you're supporting this effort by selling cake?"

"Cake is good," Mira tells me. "And cake is Natalie's passion. She's even got an online show called *Let's Bake Cake with Natalie*."

"She does?"

Mira rolls her eyes. "Do you know anything about Natalie at all?"

So if I understand correctly, Natalie's got a mission, a passion, her own cooking show, and let's not forget that she's a movie star. Meanwhile, I struggle with my math homework and eat peanut butter crackers for lunch. I wouldn't want to go to a dance with me either.

Mira presses the envelope into my hand. "Here's two hundred and twelve dollars. There's more where that came from."

I examine the wad of cash in my hand, then give it back to Mira. "Give it to her yourself."

Mira's eyes go wide. "Is Natalie coming to the pep rally tomorrow?"

I consider the small girl in front of me. Mira has been nothing but kind and caring and very, very enthusiastic since this whole roller-coaster ride with Natalie began. There is no reason for me to be annoyed with her. There is no reason for me to be annoyed with anybody. And yet.

"Listen," I say. "I'll call Natalie. I'll make sure she knows what you're doing with the cake. I'm sure that talking with you will make her happier than getting an envelope from me."

Suddenly, Mira is crying. "Danny Constantino, you are so nice."

"No," I say. "I'm not."

"You are," she insists. "And I'm just a sixth grader. And you're like an upperclassman."

"I'm in seventh grade," I say. "That is not upper-class."

"I don't care what other people say about you." Mira

throws her arms around my waist and gives me a big hug.

"What do other people say about me?"

"You're the best, Danny." Mira steps away and wipes her nose with the back of a sleeve. "Really, you're the best." She gives me a quick grin, turns, and sprints away.

"What do other people say about me?" I ask again, but it's too late. I'm left alone in the hallway, so I let myself into the office, where Gram sits studying a stack of invoices on her desk. Happily, Mr. Maggio is nowhere in sight. I drop into a chair beside my grandmother. "What do people say about me?" I ask.

"What people?" she asks without turning away from the invoices.

"I don't know," I say. "People."

"People say you're short," Gram tells me.

"I'm not short."

"I know, but people say you're short."

"What people?"

"Freakishly tall people."

"Can we go home?" I ask.

"That's the best idea I've heard all day." Gram shoves the invoices into a folder and tucks them into a drawer. Together, we make our way outside. At the Camaro, we fall into our seats as if we just got done running a marathon. Gram rubs her eyes. "I'm so tired, I actually wish you could drive today."

That perks me up. "I'll drive!"

She laughs. "I don't think so."

"Maybe you should stay home tomorrow," I suggest.

Gram shakes her head. "Tomorrow is pep rally day. Mr. Maggio will need all the help he can get."

"He could survive one day without you."

"Not pep rally day." Gram steers us through town and finally comes to a stop at my house. Before I step out of the car, she puts a hand on my arm. "Don't forget that I have to be at school very early tomorrow morning."

"Then I'll take the bus?"

Gram nods. "Sounds like a plan, Danny."

It does sound like a plan. But during the last couple weeks, most of my plans seemed to crumple around me. Still, you've got to shoot for something.

"I'll see you at school," I promise.

I hop out. Gram shifts into gear, leans over the steering wheel, and pounds on the gas pedal. The Camaro leaps forward like a fighter jet catapulting off an aircraft carrier. Just because Gram's tired doesn't mean she's slow.

Inside, I find Mom at the kitchen table. She's shoving a stack of papers into a briefcase. "Hello and goodbye," she says to me. "I'm heading to a meeting. Do you mind eating on your own tonight?"

"Campaign meeting?" I ask.

Mom swings an arm through the briefcase shoulder strap. "That's right."

I take a deep breath. "So . . . how are you feeling about the race?"

She nods. "It's looking good."

"How good?"

Mom shrugs. "Election Day will be here soon. I guess we have to wait and see."

"Really?" I say. "Do we really have to wait and see? Because it seems to me that you can't lose. You're the only one in the race."

"That's true," Mom says, "but—"

"It seems to me that you've spent all this time on a campaign that doesn't even matter. And when you're not doing that, you're running around taking care of other people's houses, or organizing other people's business, or planning other people's parades."

Mom lowers the briefcase onto a chair. "Danny—"

"And don't say you're doing it all for me. I'm not the one who wants you to be mayor. I'm the one who wants you to be my mother because right now, you don't do any more around here than Dad does. And he's dead."

Mom stares at me for a long moment. "I don't have time for this right now."

"That's not a surprise," I tell her.

"Danny," she says. "I'm sorry, but people are waiting for me. I really have to go."

I shrug. "Of course you do."

My mother crosses the room and gives me a quick kiss on the forehead. "We will talk about this later."

I'm left standing alone in the kitchen. I turn to head for my room, but a knock at the front door stops me in my tracks. I march across the living room expecting to find more goofy Natalie Flores Griffin fans on the front step. Instead, I find Natalie Flores Griffin.

"Hi," Natalie says to me.

"Hi," I reply.

So our conversation is off to a great start.

"Are you mad at me?" Natalie blurts out.

"I would have liked to go to the dance," I tell her.

"You can still go," says Natalie.

"Everybody expects me to be there with you."

"Well, I'm very sorry to disappoint everybody, Danny."

It is impossible to ignore the edge in her voice.

"Zoey and Ajay want to know if you'll be at the pep rally," I say now.

"Just Zoey and Ajay?"

"And Mira Sergiyenko. She wants to give you a bunch of money."

Natalie does not reply.

"I'll send you Ajay's number so you can call and let him know what you're doing."

"Fine," says Natalie. "Do that." She turns, rolls her bike to the sidewalk, swings a leg over the seat, and rides away.

It's possible that I could have handled the conversation just a little better.

I close the door and head for my room, where I drop onto my bed and stare at nothing. Finally, I focus on an old poster of my favorite superhero, Winnie-the-Pooh, walking hand in hand with Christopher Robin. Mom hung that poster on my wall after we learned Dad was gone. In the picture, Christopher Robin tells Pooh, "You are braver than you believe, stronger than you seem, and smarter than you think. But the most important thing is, even if we're apart . . . I'll always be with you."

It's a good poster. It's good advice from Christopher Robin too. It even helps me a little on days when I feel like Dad is especially far away. But honestly, the words seem kind of dumb when the person you're missing was standing in your yard just a minute ago. Or, even worse, when they live in the very same house as you.

Chapter 18

have a nice day

In the morning, I remember that Ajay and Zoey planned on riding to school in her dad's truck with the unicorn today. This is also the day that every kid at Cuper Cove Middle can come to school in costume. But maybe I don't want to be like every kid anymore. I dress in blue jeans, sneakers, and a T-shirt that says HAVE A NICE DAY. How's that for a future marine?

I make it to the bus stop just in time to climb aboard. Mr. Beamon sits behind the wheel in a jacket, pants, gloves, and boots that all appear to be made out of tinfoil. He's also got a pair of weird white wraparound sunglasses, and it looks like he's painted his hair and beard white too. "Spunky space pilot from the future?" I ask.

Mr. Beamon nods. "And what are you supposed to be?"

"I'm still working that out."

He offers what I guess is a space captain salute. "Carry on."

Witches, zombies, and superheroes fill almost every seat on the bus. I make my way down the aisle and finally find a spot next to a very large boy in a huge yellow rubber ducky mask. "Hey," the duck says once the bus is under way, "aren't you the seventh-grade kid going to the dance with Natalie Flores Griffin?"

"That's what people say," I tell him.

"Do you think she'd dance with an eighth-grade duck?"

I consider telling him that Natalie's teeth aren't real. Instead, I just shrug. "It couldn't hurt to ask."

At school, I find Ajay and Zoey already at my locker. They've got winged Valkyrie crowns and cardboard Spartan helmets over their heads. Nearby, Darius, Billy, and Maddie wear similar headgear. They've got cardboard armor and weapons too. "We are hoplites!" Billy announces.

"Hoplites were Ancient Greek soldiers," Darius explains.

"Highly trained Ancient Greek killing machines is more like it," says Madeline.

"Just soldiers will be fine," Ajay tells her.

"Any sign of Natalie?" I ask.

"I talked to her," says Ajay. "She's not coming. The pep rally is a mob scene even when we don't have movie stars. She's worried that somebody could get hurt."

I nod. "I understand."

By which I mean I don't understand.

In other words, I really wish Natalie were here.

Zoey pushes a Spartan helmet, armor, and a cardboard sword into my arms. "Put this on and follow us."

I strap a breastplate across my chest, shove the helmet onto my head, and slide the sword into my belt. Now I'm a hoplite too, so I fall in line with Ajay, Zoey, and Billy. Darius and Maddie take the lead with their own swords and shields. With cardboard masks covering our faces, we go unrecognized through the hallway.

"I wish we had spears," says Maddie as we maneuver through a crowd of sixth graders.

"You could hurt somebody with a spear," says Billy.

"I know." Despite her cardboard mask, I can still tell that Maddie is smiling.

Moving by the office, I see my grandmother. She is wearing a giant inflatable shark costume. "I don't care if you look just like the character in the movie," she's telling a girl with painfully short shorts, a tiny blood-stained crop top, and a baseball bat. "You can't wear that to school."

We keep going. Together, we round a corner, head down a hallway, and enter the gymnasium, where I'm surprised to find my mother talking with Mr. Maggio. Mom's wearing a gigantic periwinkle gown with pink lace angel wings tacked to the back. Plus a tiara. She's either somebody's fairy godmother or a middle-aged prom queen. Mr. Maggio is in bright blue Superman tights that might have fit him twenty years ago. I'll never look at the Man of Steel the same way again.

"Keep going," Maddie mutters. "Double time."

We pick up the pace, but not before the principal notices us. He gives a wave and shouts out a greeting. Beneath my helmet and mask, I hear something that sounds like "*Enn eetha otee oothen eetha!*"

"What did he say?" asks Billy.

"I'm sure that I don't know," says Darius.

"It's all Greek to me," says Ajay.

Maddie stops, removes her mask, and speaks to Mr. Maggio with military precision. "Requesting permission to meet Zoey's father in the parking lot behind the gym, sir."

Mr. Maggio replies in an equally official tone. "For what purpose, soldier?"

"To unload the remainder of our pep rally supplies."

Mr. Maggio places both hands on his hips and strikes a Superman pose in his blue tights. It almost looks like he's going to try and leap a tall building in a single bound. For all of our sakes, I hope he doesn't. "Did you let your homeroom teachers know where you were going?" he asks.

"We did," Maddie tells him.

I have no idea whether or not this is true.

"In that case," says Mr. Maggio, "permission is granted. And since our first bell is about to ring and the pep rally is our first activity of the day, you and your troops may remain in the gym. Rather than run around the building, please wait here for your classmates, who will join you shortly."

Maddie raises her sword in salute. "Yes, sir!"

She turns and leads us past my mother and Mr. Maggio. I'm glad I've still got my mask on. "Are those kids wearing cardboard?" I hear Mom ask.

"It's a very versatile material," Mr. Maggio tells her.

We follow Maddie and Darius toward the open set of double doors that lead to the parking lot behind our school building. In the lot, we find Zoey's dad, a short, broad-shouldered man, standing beside a giant headless unicorn and a big box truck. The truck's got a picture of a stovetop painted on the side. Beneath the stovetop, it says JIMMY ROY APPLIANCE WORLD . . . WHERE EVERY DAY IS FRY DAY!

Darius comes to a stop. He lifts his cardboard mask and stares at the unicorn body. "Is it me or is there something wrong with that unicorn?"

Mr. Roy opens a door on the truck, reaches inside, and comes out with Cooper's cardboard head. He holds it toward Darius. "Is this what you're looking for?"

Zoey steps up and takes the head. "Thanks, Dad."

"Do you need any help?" Mr. Roy asks.

Zoey shakes her head. "We'll attach the head inside."

In fact, we don't have any choice. Even without a head, getting Cooper into the building is going to be a tight squeeze.

"Sounds good." Mr. Roy leans forward, gives Zoey a high five, then hops into his truck and drives away.

"Is every day really fry day?" says Darius.

"Only if coronary disease and congestive heart failure are on your things-to-do list," says Ajay.

"Isn't your father a heart doctor?" Billy asks him.

Ajay nods. "My dad says coronary disease and congestive heart failure are going to put my sister and me through college."

Billy, Maddie, Ajay, and I grab the ropes attached to our unicorn's rolling cart. Almost fully assembled, Cooper is heavier than I expected, but together, we pull and lift and drag her from the parking lot, onto the sidewalk, through the doorway, and into the gym. We have to stand on a chair to slide her head with its golden toilet plunger horn into place.

"Nice neck," I say to Darius.

"It was just math," he says, but I can tell that he's proud of his work.

Ajay and Zoey fasten everything together with duct tape. "It's done," Ajay says. "It's really done."

The day's opening bell must have rung when we were

outside, because costumed kids are starting to file into the gym. A few of them have decorated wagons and wheelbarrows and small carts for this weekend's Halloween parade. Nobody's got anything like Cooper the Trojan Unicorn.

"Everything is in place," says Zoey.

"Not everything," I say. "Natalie's not here."

Ajay puts one more piece of duct tape over a loose piece of cardboard. "I wouldn't worry about that."

"It's fine," I say. "It's not like she wanted to be here."

"She definitely wants to be here," Zoey tells me.

"Then where is she?" I ask.

"She'll be with us soon enough," says Ajay.

Zoey shoots him a look.

"For the parade," he clarifies.

"But not for the dance," I say.

"Danny," says Ajay, "could you just forget about Natalie Flores Griffin for a minute, and enjoy the pep rally?"

"You want me to forget about Natalie Flores Griffin?" I ask.

Ajay nods, which makes his cardboard helmet bob back and forth like a carnival doll.

"You realize that Natalie Flores Griffin is all I've been thinking about ever since Asha started this whole thing."

"What does Asha have to do with anything?" says Maddie.

"I didn't invite Natalie to Cuper Cove," I explain. "Asha stole my phone and pretended to be me. Asha's the one that asked Natalie to come. Asha's the one that sent the invitation. I never wanted to go to the Halloween dance in the first place."

"That's a lie," says Ajay. He raises his voice. "Danny Constantino is lying!"

"Don't get me wrong," I say. "I hoped it would be fun, but it's mostly been crazy and even kind of stupid. I thought Natalie and I could be friends again, but I'm worried about learning how to dance, and she's figuring out how to solve world hunger."

"Danny," says Zoey, "Natalie doesn't care if you can't dance."

I shake my head. "All I'm saying is that I knew this was a bad idea from the start. Now I have a stomach-ache all the time. I definitely don't think Natalie's having fun."

"Maybe you shouldn't have asked her in the first place," says Maddie.

"Are you listening to me?" I shout. "I didn't ask her in the first place!"

Meanwhile, dozens of sixth, seventh, and eighth graders pour into the gym. As kids spot our giant unicorn, they erupt into screams and cheers. With the way everything echoes inside the gymnasium, I can barely hear myself think.

"Danny," says Ajay. "You've always wanted to go out with Natalie."

"Not like this!" I holler.

On the other side of the gym, my giant shark grandmother is working with a couple teachers to corral a rowdy group of boys who are all dressed as monsters. Mr. Maggio and Mom stand in the center of the mob and scan the room nervously as if they're waiting for someone to show up. I know who they're waiting for.

"I wanted to go out on a date with a girl I liked," I tell my friends. "But I'm not even her date. I'm 'Hashtag What-was-she-thinking.'"

"Danny," says Zoey. "It's not like that."

I shake my head. "That is exactly what it's like."

Ajay takes a step toward me. "You're wrong," he says, "and you really need to shut up."

I raise my cardboard sword and turn on Ajay. "Don't tell me to shut up."

That's when my mother's amplified voice fills the room. "Boys and girls," she says sweetly. "Let's settle down and find a seat. This is a big day, and we are expecting a very special guest." Apparently she travels with her own microphone now.

"You don't get it," I shout at my friends.

Suddenly, the backside of our cardboard unicorn bursts open. The long rope tail attached to the secret hatchway whacks the side of my head. It knocks the helmet and mask off my face just in time for me to see Natalie step out of her hiding place inside Cooper the Trojan Unicorn.

"And here she is!" says Mom, who is almost as shocked as I am.

"I tried to tell you," says Ajay. "Natalie called last night. I convinced her to come to the pep rally."

"We wanted it to be a surprise," says Zoey.

"I am surprised," I admit.

Natalie hops off the unicorn platform and onto the gym floor. She approaches me, leans close, and whispers into my ear, "Tell Asha I'm very sorry that I can't be the date she was hoping for."

I don't know how to respond. For better or worse, it doesn't matter. Because right then is when the screaming begins.

Chapter 19

cooper the trojan unicorn is dead

"Stay calm!" Mom yells into her microphone. "Everybody, just stay calm."

I turn to see what's going on. Kids who had been seated on the floor near the gymnasium's exit doors are trying to back away from something on the ground. Others push forward for a better look. "What's happening?" I say.

"Danny," Natalie says. "It's your grandmother."

I look around the room. Gram is nowhere to be seen, which is confusing because she's usually the first one to wade into any kind of commotion. Also, she's wearing a giant inflatable shark costume.

"Don't worry." Natalie pulls out her cell phone. "I'm calling 911."

"For what?"

Before anybody can answer, there is another scream, plus the sound of a giant *POP!*

Now the big rubber ducky I met on the bus is trying to stand on tiptoe to see what's going on. Pushing into the crowd, he trips and stumbles toward our unicorn. Darius rushes forward to prevent the unsteady duck from a crash. Unfortunately, Darius is a much better soldier than a crossing guard. Rather than prop up the dumb duck, Darius whacks him with his cardboard dagger. Startled, the duck turns and punches Darius in the chest. Now they're both off balance and waving their arms like geese wrapped up in an electric fence.

"Look out!" I shout, but it's too late. The two boys stagger into Cooper like half-cocked battering rams.

"Danny!" Ajay grabs my arm. "Don't worry about that! Your grandmother fell down. She's lying on the floor." He points across the room. "Let's go."

I tear off my cardboard armor and try to make my way to Gram, but the crowd is too thick. "Let us pass!" shouts Maddie. She begins whacking kids with her own cardboard weapon and shoving them aside with her shield. It's not the most graceful solution, but it works.

A moment later, I'm at Gram's side. Mom's there too. "Give her some air!" Mom yells at the circle of kids around us. "Give her some air!"

"I don't need any more air," Gram snaps. "That's what got me into this mess."

"What are you talking about?" says Mom.

Gram moves to a sitting position. She raises a hand to show us a deflated shark costume hanging off her arm. "I overinflated. Then I couldn't see where I was going. I tripped, and I popped."

"Can you stand?" I ask her.

She shakes her head. "I hurt my ankle." She closes her eyes. "Actually, I think I broke my ankle."

A siren wails in the distance, but it's getting closer quickly. Mom and Maddie push the crowd of kids back. From there, Mr. Maggio and the rest of our teachers move students toward the door and start marching them back to class. By the time the ambulance arrives, the gym is mostly empty. For just a moment, it's only me, Mom, Mr. Maggio, and Natalie with Gram, who's leaning against a wall now.

"I'm really sorry," I say to Natalie, who is kneeling beside me.

She gives a quick nod. "You should be."

"You really should be," Mom adds.

"I'm not talking to you," I tell my mother.

"There's no need to apologize," Gram mumbles. She's still got her eyes closed. "I did this to myself."

"That's not what I'm apologizing for," I tell my grandmother.

Gram opens her eyes. "Then what—"

Before she can finish, paramedics burst into the

room with equipment carts, oxygen tanks, and a rolling stretcher. One of them, a stocky, round-faced woman, approaches quickly. She's got a stethoscope around her neck, a walkie-talkie on her belt, and one arm completely covered in floral tattoos. The tattooed lady moves us out of the way while she assesses the situation. With very little delay, she cuts the shark costume off Gram. "My dad and I go deep-sea fishing," the woman tells us. "Believe it or not, this is not the weirdest thing I've ever found inside a shark."

I don't even want to know.

The paramedics lift Gram, strap her to a stretcher, and start moving to the door. "Meet me at the hospital," Gram hollers back.

"Got it," says Mom, and races out the door. Mr. Maggio follows. I turn to speak to Natalie, but she must have slipped away during all the commotion. Now I'm standing alone.

Around me, the gym floor is littered with pieces of Halloween candy and costume parts. I step over a cardboard sword and a few remaining shards from Gram's plastic shark. Nearby, our Halloween masterpiece lies crumpled on her side. By any measure, Cooper the Trojan Unicorn is dead. She is battered and broken and alone. I know exactly how she feels. If Zoey were here, she'd almost certainly feel compelled to tell me that I have finally reached my dark night of the soul. I am glad that Zoey is not here right now.

Suddenly, the gymnasium doors swing open. Mom stands in the entryway. "Danny," she says, "what are you waiting for?"

"I thought you left without me."

"Don't be ridiculous," says Mom. "I brought the car around. Let's go."

I have to jog to catch up. Outside, I find Mom sitting behind the wheel of Gram's car. I open the passenger door and drop into my seat. Before I can speak, Mom punches the gas and peels out of the parking lot. "Are you allowed to drive Gram's Camaro?" I ask.

Out in the street, she blasts through a yellow light and then points us toward the hospital. "I learned how to drive in this car. One day, you will too."

"Not if you kill us both before I turn sixteen."

"Sorry." Mom lets up on the gas just a little. "I'm running on adrenaline right now."

"How is this different from every other day?"

"My angel wings aren't usually this visible." She shoots me a quick look. "What happened back there between you and Natalie?"

I shake my head. "I said something stupid."

"Like mother like son, huh?"

Mom passes a slow-moving minivan on a long

straightaway, then cuts the wheel to take a tight turn. She drifts a little too close to the shoulder of the road and clips several sidewalk scarecrows holding MISSY FOR MAYOR signs. This particular group is dressed up like characters from *The Wizard of Oz*. I'm happy to see Dorothy, the Tin Man, and the Cowardly Lion all explode in a cloud of straw.

"I hate that movie," Mom mutters.

Finally, Mom downshifts, makes a couple more turns, and then brings us onto the Cuper Cove Hospital driveway. Approaching the entrance, Mom slows to a crawl in search of a parking spot. Seeing none, she makes the sign of the cross. "Mother Cabrini, Mother Cabrini, please find a spot for my little machiney."

She really does have a prayer for everything. "You realize that's ridiculous, right?"

"And yet," she says, "it never fails."

A moment later, a space opens up. Mom parks, and I open the door to get out. My mother puts a hand on my arm and stops me. "Danny, I want to talk to you."

"Gram is waiting," I remind her. "We can talk later."

She grips my arm tighter. "She just hurt her ankle."

"And got bitten by a shark."

"She's not going to die," Mom says.

"Thanks to one of your dumb prayers?"

"They're not dumb to me," Mom snaps. "And if you

must know, I started praying the minute I saw your grandmother on the floor. It wouldn't hurt if you said a few prayers yourself."

I turn to face Mom. "I've been praying you won't be mayor, but I don't think that prayer's going to be answered."

"Just because you don't get what you ask for doesn't mean your prayer doesn't get answered," Mom tells me.

I cross my arms. "Why did you have to do a big complicated campaign anyway?"

"A campaign is how you tell people what you want and how you want it," she tells me.

"Oh," I say. "In that case, you're always in a campaign."

She laughs like she just figured something out. "Danny, everybody's always in a campaign."

"I'm not."

"You're kidding, right?"

"What are you talking about?" I say.

"Danny," says Mom. "You're in a campaign to make your mother want to kill you. You're in a campaign to fill my house with weird drawings of mutant super weirdos. You're in a campaign to make Natalie Flores Griffin like you. And by the way, I hear that last one seems to be going pretty well."

"No thanks to you," I tell my mother.

"Because I made her behave like a movie star? News

flash, Danny. Natalie Flores Griffin is an actual movie star."

"News flash," I tell my mom. "Nobody comes to Cuper Cove to be a movie star."

Mom glances in the Camaro's rearview mirror and fixes her tiara. "Tell me about it."

"Natalie came to Cuper Cove so she could be normal for a change, and you ruined it. She wanted to go to a school dance and then go trick-or-treating and then eat too much candy and then go home. That's it. Why couldn't you let her have that?"

"Danny," says Mom, "you just listed all the things that *you* want."

"And because of all the things that *you* want, none of it is going to come true for me either."

"Do you know why I get the things I want?" Mom asks me now.

"Because you're bossy and loud and you always think you're right?"

"Because I go for it," Mom says.

"What do you mean?" I ask.

Mom looks me in the eye. "Figure it out."

"Fine," I say. "I will." I step out of the Camaro and slam the door behind me.

Chapter 20

a visual and terrible revelation of truth

Thanks to Mother Cabrini and the miracle of the perfect parking space, the hospital entrance is just a few feet away. I march inside, where I find a white-haired nurse seated at a reception desk. "I'm looking for my grandmother," I say. "I think she broke her ankle."

"Broken ankles go to the Emergency Room," the nurse tells me. "That's on the other side of the building."

"How do I get there from here?"

She points at a set of double doors directly behind her. "Up. Up. Down. Down. Left. Right. Left. Right. Then take the B elevator to the A level. Got it?"

"Up. Up. Down. Down. Left. Right. Left. Right. B. A," I repeat.

"Got it," she says. "You'll be there in no time."

I rush into a zigzag maze of long hospital corridors. Somehow, I follow the directions and find myself at the Emergency Room waiting area. I stop to let a team of paramedics roll a patient from an ambulance into the building. I peek at the stretcher and see a guy with an arrow sticking out of his shoulder. "What are you looking at?" he asks me.

"You're not my grandmother," I tell him.

"Good thing for her," the man says.

"Danny!" calls a familiar voice.

I turn and see Mr. Beamon entering the hospital. He's easy to pick out because he's still wearing most of his spunky space pilot costume. Plus he's a lot taller when he's not seated behind a school bus steering wheel. A moment later, Ajay and Zoey along with Darius, Billy, and Maddie rush inside too. Maddie's still got a winged helmet on her head. It's battered and torn, which makes her look even tougher than usual. "How did you get here?" I say.

"We know a man who drives a bus," says Maddie.

"Your mom texted me," Mr. Beamon explains. "She told me to pick up this crew and get over here right away. You might not know this," he adds, "but your mother is very good at giving orders."

Tell me about it. "Can we please find my grandmother?" I say.

With Mr. Beamon's help, we learn that Gram has been moved to something called the Acute Medical Unit on the hospital's sixth floor. According to a nurse at the

Emergency Room desk, only two people at a time can visit Acute Medical Unit patients. Not only that, all Acute Medical Unit visitors must be adults. "Thank you," Mr. Beamon says to the nurse. "We understand."

"We do?" I say.

He nods, takes us a few steps away from the nurse's station, and then whispers, "*Listen, smile, agree, and then do whatever you were gonna do anyway.*"

"That's a line from *Iron Man*," I tell him.

"It is," Mr. Beamon confirms.

"But Iron Man's got a super high-tech exoskeleton with sentient armor, onboard proton beams, guided missiles, and supersonic flight capability," says Ajay. "What have we got?"

Mr. Beamon holds out both arms to show off his tinfoil suit. "A spunky space pilot from the future and his ragtag group of rule-breaking rebels."

We seriously have the best school bus driver in the world.

Mr. Beamon leads my friends and me out of the busy Emergency Room. Together, we head toward the yellow school bus parked at the curb.

"How were you able to find a parking spot so close to the hospital?" I ask Mr. Beamon.

"Mother Cabrini, Mother Cabrini, please find a spot for my little machiney," he tells me.

I should have known.

We sneak behind the bus, then follow Ajay, who leads us down a sidewalk to another entrance. "Where are we going?" Darius asks.

"Don't worry," Zoey says. "Ajay's parents work here. He knows what he's doing." She reaches out, takes Ajay's hand, and gives it a quick squeeze. The gesture is so easy and natural that I barely give it a thought. But then something strikes me.

"Hey," I say, "are you two—"

Zoey holds up her free hand. "Let's focus on your grandmother."

We reenter the hospital building. Ajay brings us to a single tiny elevator at the end of a long, empty corridor. All seven of us cram inside. Somebody punches a button, and we're on our way to the sixth floor. "Can anybody spell *claustrophobia*?" asks Mr. Beamon.

"C," says Billy. "L . . ."

Mr. Beamon closes his eyes. "I was kidding."

Billy stops, and we ride the rest of the way in silence. The quiet is kind of shocking after the morning I've had so far. In the last few hours, I've pretended to be a Greek warrior, witnessed the death of a cardboard unicorn, insulted a Hollywood movie starlet, run over Dorothy and her friends from Oz, and watched my grandmother get cut out of a shark. And it's not even lunchtime yet.

The elevator finally slows to a stop. After a long moment, the doors slide open. Mr. Beamon releases an extended sigh. "Were you holding your breath?" Maddie asks him.

"All I'm going to say is this." Mr. Beamon massages the sides of his head with both hands. "If we can't find a stairway leading out, then I have to live here now."

Ajay brings us down one more long hallway. "We're almost there," he promises.

Rounding a final corner, we see a small sign pointing toward the Acute Medical Unit. Together, we follow an arrow, head through a swinging door, and then nearly crash right into my mother. She's standing in the middle of a wide-open corridor lined with doorways covered by blue-and-white privacy curtains. Mom's angel wings are crumpled. Her tiara is gone, and she's speaking with Ajay's parents.

"The ankle will heal quickly," Dr. Kalli tells Mom. "And if Ms. Constantino can control her blood pressure, manage her cholesterol levels, avoid fried foods, and limit her salt intake, it is likely that she will not die for many years."

"What he means," says Mrs. Kalli, "is that Danny's grandmother is going to be fine."

"My dad is a surgeon," Ajay whispers. "Mom says he doesn't communicate well with people who are actually awake."

Our parents turn and see us standing in the hallway. "Is Gram okay?" I ask.

Dr. Kalli approaches and offers me an awkward pat on the shoulder. "Don't worry, Danny," he says. "A full recovery is very probable."

"She's going to be fine," Mrs. Kalli promises.

I look at my mother. Her cheeks are covered with black mascara lines. "Have you been crying?"

She nods. "I got lost in the hospital." She pats her head. "And I lost my tiara."

This is usually the part where Mom would say "Dear Saint Anthony, please come around. Something is lost and cannot be found." But she must really be upset, because she just keeps talking.

"And I was worried about you. And of course your grandmother. But mostly you. I didn't want to get in a fight today, Danny."

"You started it," I mutter.

She takes a step back. "Do you really want to do this here?" she asks.

As a matter of fact, I do.

"Why do you have to be the mayor?" I say to my mother. "Isn't being queen of everything enough?"

Before Mom can respond, Madeline MacSweeney steps up from behind and pokes me with her cardboard sword. "What's wrong with you?" she says. "Your mother is going to be a great mayor."

"I'd like her to be a great mom."

"Guess what," Mom says to me. "I'd like that too." She straightens her wings and adjusts her dress so that it hangs properly on her shoulders. "I'd also like to be a great mayor and a great real estate agent, and I'd like to lead a great Halloween parade. I'm sorry if I'm not living up to your standards, Danny. But last time I checked, I am allowed to be more than one thing at a time."

I glance at Mr. Beamon for help, but he raises his hands and takes a step back. "I fought and died on this hill a long time ago."

"What's that supposed to mean?" Mom says to him.

"Does Danny know?" he asks.

"Know what?" I say.

"Excuse me," a nurse calls to us from behind a nearby desk. "This is not the family counseling department. You're all going to have to move to a waiting room."

"I asked your mother to marry me once," Mr. Beamon shares.

The nurse's eyes go wide. "But first," she says, "I'd like to hear how this all works out." She points at Mr. Beamon. "Go on."

"You know we dated in high school," he tells me. "After your dad died, I used to come over to check on you and your mom. We became close. I even got you a dog."

Mom shakes her head. "Our house is going to smell like that dog forever."

"Jacko?" I say.

Mr. Beamon nods. "I got you a dog, and I asked your mom to marry me."

"All you ever wanted was to be a school bus driver," Mom tells him. "I wanted more."

"You wanted a marine," Mr. Beamon says gently.

"It wasn't that simple," Mom tells him.

The nurse shakes her head. "It never is." She turns to me. "So what's your problem?"

"I don't have a problem." I nod toward my mother. "She's the one with the problem."

"My problem," says Mom, "is that my son thinks I'm a monster."

Suddenly, a nearby privacy curtain flies open to reveal my grandmother. She's seated in a wheelchair and wearing a dull green hospital smock. She's got a cast on one foot and a pink ankle-high sock on the other. It is not a good look for her. "Sometimes," she announces, "we are all monsters."

"In horror movies," says Zoey, "the monster is basically a visual and terrible revelation of truth."

Everybody turns and stares at the small girl wearing a cardboard hat and cat's-eye glasses.

"Don't worry," Ajay tells us. "She just says stuff like that sometimes."

"How's the ankle?" Mr. Beamon says to Gram.

"It hurts." She nods at the tinfoil costume. "Nice

outfit. Let me guess. Spunky space pilot from the future heading into a *Battle Beyond the Stars*?"

Mr. Beamon points at me and my friends. "I even brought a motley crew of ragtag rebels."

Gram grins. "How's the bus business?"

"This is probably my last year behind the wheel," he says.

"What do you mean?" I ask.

"Are you quitting?" says Zoey.

"Did you get fired?" asks Ajay.

"He can't get fired," Gram tells us. "He owns the bus company."

"You do?" says Mom.

He shrugs. "I run a transportation empire."

"Seven school buses is not an empire," Gram tells him.

"And three vans," Mr. Beamon says.

Gram rolls her eyes. "They're minivans."

"That sounds like an empire to me." The nurse turns to my mother. "This man is a catch. Are you still single?"

"Enough," says Dr. Kalli. "Ms. Constantino needs to rest."

"I really do," says Mom.

"He's not talking about you," I whisper.

"Everybody follow me," Mrs. Kalli announces. "Today is Thursday, and that means fresh chocolate chip cookies in the cafeteria. My treat."

My friends head down the hall with Ajay's mom. Zoey reaches out and takes Mr. Beamon's hand. "We can take the stairs."

I stand, unsure whether I should stay or go.

"Danny," says Mom. "I'd like to sit and talk with your grandmother for a minute."

"Without me?" I ask.

"Just for a minute," she says. "But maybe you could bring us back a couple of those cookies."

I nod. "I'll be right back," I promise.

Chapter 21

there is no such thing as a good fish stick

Sometimes a group of seventh graders is like a sack of grasshoppers. That's what Gram says. We're all motion and noise. Plus we're kind of gross. And according to the Bible, we might be a plague. Also, we eat a lot, so bringing us to a cafeteria is a very good idea. Still, I drift away from my friends once I get my cookies. Sometimes even a grasshopper needs a little time alone.

I sit at a table near a window and look outside at a cold, gray sky. I hope it doesn't rain on tomorrow's parade. Rain or shine, the Halloween parade route ends at the school so kids can move straight into the gym for the Friday night dance. I'm pretty sure I won't be there. Now that I think about it, I don't even have a costume anymore, so Saturday night trick-or-treating is out of the picture too.

Behind me, a chair scrapes across the floor while somebody takes a seat at a nearby table. I turn to see if one of my friends has decided to invade my space. Instead, I find Natalie Flores Griffin.

"Do you mind if I sit?" she says.

"What are you doing here?" I ask.

"I was worried about your grandmother." She places a tray on her table. "And I was worried about you. Also, I'm obsessed with cafeteria food." She offers me a paper box filled with something that's fried, breaded, and shaped like a bunch of short squished candles. "Want a fish stick?"

"I hate fish sticks."

"My parents say I cried about missing Cuper Cove cafeteria fish sticks for a month after we moved to California."

"I thought you hated fish sticks too."

She shrugs. "For a while, going to cafeterias was like a family thing for us. In between auditions and rehearsals and dance classes and acting lessons, we'd go hunting for the perfect fish stick. Sometimes, we'd drop by a nice school somewhere around Los Angeles. My parents would tell the principal or the headmaster that we were house shopping and wanted to learn what the neighborhood school had to offer. We'd usually get a quick tour, and then we'd eat lunch in the cafeteria, which was the only point."

"That's kind of funny."

"That's how I learned that school cafeterias need some serious help."

"And that's why you started your foundation?"

Natalie shakes her head. "My publicists and financial

advisors recommended that we give some of my money away. Giving kids food that's not gross seemed like a good cause."

I try not to obsess over the fact that Natalie has publicists and financial advisors. "Did you ever find any good fish sticks?"

"Danny," Natalie says to me, "there is no such thing as a good fish stick."

"So you do hate fish sticks?"

"Always did. Always will. I just missed sharing them with you and the squirrels." She stands, discards the box of greasy food, and takes a chair at my table.

"Did you really come to Cuper Cove just because I asked you?"

"You didn't ask me," she points out.

I forgot that she knew about that. "I'm sorry," I say. "I always wanted to. I just thought it would be weird."

"I think you may have been right."

Neither of us speaks for a long moment.

"I'm glad you're here now," I finally say.

Natalie slides her chair a little closer. "Me too."

"But what about *Sidewalk Scarecrows*?" I ask.

Natalie looks confused. "My mom's movie?"

"My mother says it's your movie. She says you're just here to use Cuper Cove for publicity."

Natalie leans back and crosses her arms. "*Sidewalk*

Scarecrows is a documentary. You'll never guess what it's about."

"What?"

"Scarecrows," Natalie tells me.

"Like actual scarecrows?"

Natalie nods. "My mom is obsessed with them. She says it's because she grew up surrounded by scarecrows in Cuper Cove. Last year, she put a small film crew together, and they went all over the world talking to people about—"

"Scarecrows?"

"Exactly. And Cuper Cove definitely plays a big part, but *Sidewalk Scarecrows* is no blockbuster. They're going to show it next year on some Internet travel channel. All the publicity in the world isn't going to change the Rotten Tomatoes score on that one."

"Sorry," I say. "Sometimes my mother . . ."

"She's got a strong personality," Natalie offers.

"You noticed?"

"My mother has made Quentin Tarantino and Dwayne The Rock Johnson cry," Natalie tells me. "I recognize the type."

The two of us sit quietly and stare outside at a hint of blue peeking through October clouds. "My grandmother is going to be okay," I tell Natalie.

"I know," she says.

"I'm sorry about the things I said in the gym."

"I know," she says once more.

"It's just—"

Natalie interrupts. "I didn't want you to see me like that."

"Like what?"

"Like a person you only know from the movies."

"But that's part of who you are," I say. "You're a movie star."

"Being in a movie doesn't feel like being a star," she tries to explain. "It just feels like playing. Later, people who actually know what they're doing put it all together. If the writing is good and the lighting is good and the editing is good and a million other things that have nothing to do with me are good, then people think I'm brilliant. If not, people go online and call me names. Either way, I just happen to be there when they're taking the pictures."

"I don't think you're giving yourself enough credit."

"I'm sorry I can't go to the dance," she says now.

"Is your mom really afraid that it could turn into a madhouse?"

"Were you at the pep rally today?" Natalie asks.

"That wasn't your fault," I point out.

"But it could have been. And I would hate if somebody got hurt because—"

"Because you are a movie star," I say.

Natalie nods. "But this isn't a movie," she tells me.

"There is no script. There is no map. There are no stars. If it is possible, we will find our way together."

I study Natalie's face. "Isn't that a line from *Mutant Zombie Soul Pirates?*" I ask.

"It is," she admits. "But it's a good one. Do you remember what comes next?"

"Isn't that when you—"

Natalie leans forward and gives me a quick, soft kiss on the lips. "Yes."

I feel my face burn red.

"I think that was even better than the one in the movie," she tells me.

"The movie was animated," I remind her.

Natalie stands. "I have to go."

"When do you leave for California?" I ask.

Suddenly, Natalie looks small and uncomfortable. "My mom is trying to get a flight for tonight."

I feel as if all the air has rushed out of my lungs. "Why?"

"Filming is back on schedule. The director wants to shoot a scene with me the day after tomorrow. Since I'm not going to the dance, and I don't want to be the Halloween queen, my mom says we can get home so I have a day to rest."

"But—"

"But we can still talk on the phone," she says.

"Okay," I get out. "I'd like that."

Without warning, Natalie steps forward, wraps me up in a quick hug, and then runs out the nearest door.

I don't know if I will ever see her again. I don't know if I can wipe the tears out of my eyes before I have to face my friends. But I do know one thing. Natalie Flores Griffin says I'm a better kisser than a cartoon pirate. That's not nothing. And it definitely takes a little bit of the sting off of a long, hard day.

Chapter 22

a dark night of the soul is sort of inevitable

On Friday night, Mom and I sit in Gram's hospital room and watch an old movie called *Corpse Bride*. It's an animated story about a boy who's supposed to marry a girl he's never met, but then that goes wrong and he accidentally marries a different girl who just happens to be dead.

And I thought I had problems.

The movie is a good Halloween choice even though it's not very scary. Actually, it's kind of sweet and even a little sad because the boy and both girls—the living one and the dead one—are really very nice. And the boy likes them both. No matter what he does, somebody is going to get hurt. We're well into the movie when I realize something. "This is a romantic comedy."

Gram laughs. "Everything is a romantic comedy, Danny."

I point at the television set mounted above the foot of Gram's hospital bed. "All these characters are going to face a dark night of the soul."

"Half the people in this movie are corpses," says Mom. "A dark night of the soul is sort of inevitable."

"Everybody will have to sacrifice something," I say. "Everybody is going to lose, but it will be a joyful defeat because . . ."

"Because there's kissing," says Gram.

"Because there's true love," I tell her.

Mom turns to look at me. "What do you know about true love?"

"Zoey explained it to me."

Gram shifts in her hospital bed. She's really ready to go home. "Did Zoey end up taking Ajay to the dance?"

I nod. "That's where they are now."

Gram holds out her hand. "I won that bet."

Mom digs into her purse, finds a five-dollar bill, and hands it over.

On-screen a few minutes later, the dead girl in the bride's dress returns a wedding ring to the boy so he can pursue his true love. "You kept your promise," she tells him. "You set me free. Now I can do the same for you."

Mom dabs at her eyes. "I love this part."

"Have you seen this before?" I ask.

"It's a rom-com," she says. "Of course I've seen it before."

I'm not sure if she means *Corpse Bride* or if she means any final scene that includes happy kissing, eternal vows, and true love.

"Are you going to call Mr. Beamon?" I ask once the movie credits have come and gone.

"Funny you should ask," says Mom. "He called earlier today wondering if we might get together for a cup of coffee."

"What did you say?"

"It's just coffee," Mom tells me.

"Is that a yes?" Gram asks.

"Yes," Mom says to Gram and me. "I am going to meet Shad Beamon for a cup of coffee."

Gram nods. "And I won that bet too."

I dig into a pocket, find a five-dollar bill, and hand it to my grandmother.

The following morning, we help Gram back into her own house. "I think you should stay with us for a few days," Mom tells her.

My grandmother, still in a wheelchair, rolls into the kitchen to check on her plants. Her favorites are lined up neatly along a window ledge above the sink. "The doctor says I'm supposed to rest for a few days. I can do that here."

"What about Halloween?" I ask.

Gram pulls herself to a standing position at the counter, fills a measuring cup in the sink, and begins pouring water into each plant. "What about it?"

"It's tonight," I remind her. "Trick-or-treaters will start ringing your doorbell before the sun goes down."

Gram stops, closes her eyes, and takes a deep breath. "I forgot about that. I never even bought any candy."

"We've got plenty," says Mom. "How about I come and get you for supper? You can help Danny and me hand things out, and then I'll bring you home when the night is over."

"Aren't you going trick-or-treating with your friends?" Gram asks me.

"I'd rather stay with you," I tell her.

"Are you afraid I'm going somewhere?"

I shrug.

"I'm not going to die from a broken ankle," she promises.

"You have other risk factors," I tell her. "You're supposed to control your blood pressure, manage your cholesterol levels, stay away from fried foods, limit your salt intake, and avoid inflatable sharks. And," I add, "there might be sharks."

Gram rolls her eyes.

"I want to help," I say.

"Plus," says Mom, "Danny doesn't have a costume."

After a surprisingly limited protest, Gram agrees to join us for dinner and trick-or-treating. I suspect her ankle must still hurt a lot.

Later, she parks her wheelchair just inside our front door so she can greet trick-or-treaters. The first group includes three Raggedy Anns, two ballerinas, one witch, and a goat. The goat is not in a costume. It's an actual goat. One of the ballerinas holds the animal on a leash. "He likes marshmallows," she tells us.

Gram gives the goat a box of marshmallow Peeps. The goat eats the Peeps and the cardboard box too. "Kid tested," Gram says. "Nanny goat approved."

The next time the bell rings, I find my friends standing on our doorstep. Billy, Maddie, Darius, Zoey, and Ajay are dressed like Greek soldiers. They've fully repaired and repainted their cardboard helmets and armor, and they look great.

"*Fársa í kérasma!*" Maddie yells at me.

I turn to Ajay, who is holding hands with Zoey. "Did she just call me a name?"

"It's 'trick-or-treat'!" Maddie explains. "In Greek!"

"At least according to Google," says Zoey.

Gram and Mom join me at the door, and we pour candy into my friends' bags. It's obvious that the whole group is more than a little sugared up already. Before I know it they've all said thank you and goodbye and Happy Halloween, and now they're gone.

"Are you sure you don't want to join them?" Gram asks after we close the door.

"I'm exactly where I want to be," I tell her.

The bell rings again.

"I've got it," says Mom. She swings the door open and stares at a lone trick-or-treater carrying a giant plastic pumpkin and wearing a costume that neither one of us recognizes. It's a furry brown body with fat matching mittens, a long brown tail, and feet that look like paws. At the same time, the head belongs to an eagle, with feathery white ears and a bright yellow beak. Plus, it's got wings. "What are you supposed to be?" Mom asks.

Gram leans forward to get a better look. "That's a griffin."

"A griffin?" says Mom.

"The body of a lion with the head and wings of an eagle," Gram explains. "Definitely a griffin."

The trick-or-treater nods, then puts both paws on the eagle beak and tries to lift it off. After a moment's struggle, it's clear that the mask is stuck. I step forward to help. After some awkward wrestling, the eagle head pops off revealing a sweaty, red-faced Natalie Flores Griffin.

"Griffin," I say. "I get it."

Natalie wipes a feathered arm across her face. "It's really hot in there."

Gram waves from her chair. "Happy Halloween, Natalie!"

"How are you feeling?" Natalie asks my grandmother.

"Like I broke my ankle," says Gram. "Otherwise, I'm good."

Natalie gives Gram a big smile, then turns to me. "Are you surprised?"

"Yes," I say. "But I'm getting used to being surprised by you."

"What happened to your movie schedule?" asks Mom.

"We convinced them to push it back a day," Natalie explains. "Because every once in a while, the movie star gets to have things her way."

Mom grins. "I can appreciate that."

Natalie glances around the living room, then sniffs. "It doesn't smell like smoke in here anymore."

"With luck," says Gram, "Missy Constantino will never cook again."

"Mayors don't cook," says Mom.

"Then you've got my vote," Gram tells her.

Natalie smiles and laughs, and suddenly I do not want to sit inside my house on Halloween night. "Since you're here," I say to Natalie, "and since you're in a costume . . ."

Natalie clasps her hands together and almost starts jumping up and down. "Are you going to ask to take me trick-or-treating? Are you?"

"If you let me finish my sentence."

"Yes!" she says. "I would love to go trick-or-treating with you, Danny!"

"I don't have a costume," I confess. "But we can still walk together."

Natalie reaches into her plastic pumpkin and pulls out a paper tiger mask. "Asha said I should give this to you."

"You were at the Kallis' house?"

"Just a few minute ago," she tells me. "Ajay, Zoey, and everybody are waiting for us outside."

I peek out the window. Five small Greek soldiers wave back at me.

Natalie presses the tiger mask into my hands.

"You want me to go as a paper tiger?" I ask.

"Danny Constantino," says Natalie, "you are not a paper tiger. You are Cuper Cove's first Pulikali dancer."

Even though it's just a simple paper plate decorated with orange and black stripes plus a couple eye holes, the mask looks great. It's really well put together too. It even has a long Velcro strap, which I wrap around the back of my head. Thank you, Asha Kalli.

I hold out my arm. "Would you like to go trick-or-treating with me?" I say to Natalie.

She grins. "Are you asking me on a date?"

I glance at Gram and Mom. Their heads nod up and down like rocking chairs on rocket fuel.

"Yes," I say. "I am."

"In that case," says Natalie, "I am very pleased to accept your invitation."

I help Natalie get back into her eagle head. She reaches out and puts her paw in mine. "This is my first real date ever."

"Mine too," I admit.

With Mom's help, we maneuver through the door and back outside. I lead Natalie across the yard. Despite her eagle eyes, she can barely see a thing in that mask. We join our friends on the sidewalk and head into the night. Natalie stumbles, but I've got her arm, so I hold her up.

"What's the plan for making this work?" she asks.

I smile beneath my tiger mask and give her paw a squeeze. "We'll figure it out as we go."

Chapter 23

the definition of an epilogue

Cuper Cove's Election Day comes just three days after Halloween. I slip into my room and phone Natalie as soon as the results are in. "My mother is Cuper Cove's new mayor," I tell her.

"Isn't that what you expected?" she asks.

It's quiet behind Natalie, so I know that she's at home. I've learned that she and her mom share a pretty apartment around the corner from something called the La Brea Tar Pits. These are basically huge holes filled with smelly, molten, naturally occurring liquid asphalt. Over tens of thousands of years, ancient wolves, woolly mammoths, giant sloths, and more have been trapped and died in the pits. It's hard to believe that this is a nice neighborhood, but Natalie promises I'll like it when I visit one day. Right now, California just sounds weird.

"I was hoping for a miracle," I say.

Natalie laughs. "I don't think that's what miracles are for, Danny."

I lie back on my bed. "My mom's boyfriend says the same thing."

"Your mother has a boyfriend?"

"It's a new development."

Mr. Beamon—he says I can call him Shad when we're not on the bus—is downstairs preparing pumpkin soup, fresh bread, and homemade apple pie so we can share a victory dinner for Mom at Gram's house tomorrow. It's going to be just the four of us.

"I think it's going to be good," I say.

"I'm glad," says Natalie. "Do you have time to help me with some homework?" she asks now.

"Sure," I say. "What have you got?"

"What is a good example of an epilogue?"

I move over to my computer and look up the definition of the word.

"Epilogue," I say. "*Noun. A concluding part added to a novel, film, or play, which often gives a short statement about what happens to the characters after the story finishes. It comes from the Greek word epi, which means 'in addition' and logos, which means 'word.'*"

"You speak Greek?" says Natalie.

"I speak Wikipedia," I tell her.

"I know the last bit at the end of the final Harry Potter movie is an epilogue," says Natalie. "But I hate that one."

"Why?" I ask.

"They all just live happily ever after."

"What's wrong with happily ever after?"

"It doesn't leave anything to the imagination."

I tap at my computer. "According to the World Wide Web, *Romeo and Juliet* has an epilogue."

Natalie makes a gagging sound.

"Is it another happily ever after?" I ask.

"For never was a story of more woe," Natalie says in her theater voice. *"Than this of Juliet and her Romeo."*

On my screen, I see a pen-and-ink sketch of two sobbing teenagers. "I thought it was a romance."

"Romance it is, and yet comedy no. Please never become my own Romeo."

"Did you just make a poem?"

Natalie ignores my question. "Spoiler alert," she says. "Romeo and Juliet die in the end."

"I've got a better one," I tell her. "Have you ever seen a movie called *Up*?"

Natalie gasps. "Danny, that's my favorite movie of all time. The final three minutes are brilliant. The two main characters, Russell and Mr. Frederickson, win a fighter plane battle, they make it home for Russell's Senior Wilderness Explorer Award, they get ice cream cones, and then we know that Mr. Frederickson and Russell are going to stay friends forever. They're more like a family really. And of course, there's a talking dog."

"Of course," I say.

"Not only that," Natalie continues at breakneck speed, "Mr. Frederickson is going to live out the rest of his life in the way that his true love, Ellie, would have wanted him to. He's basically going to be his best self. Oh, I wish Ellie could have been alive to see it. Don't you?"

"Sure," I say. Though honestly, I'm having a little trouble keeping up.

"And speaking of Ellie, in the very, very last seconds of the movie, we see Ellie's house is now on a cliff overlooking Paradise Falls, and that's what she always wanted since she was a little girl. So even though she's dead, her dreams can all still come true."

"Wow," I say. "You really like *Up* a lot."

Natalie sighs. "It's perfect."

"I don't remember all of that happening in the last three minutes."

"It's all there," she assures me. "It's like a giant promise that even though it's really hard, people can keep each other honest and true and good. They can stay together, and they can love each other." She pauses and then adds, "Wouldn't it be amazing if that happened to us?"

I think of the long road Mr. Beamon—Shad—had to travel before he ended up downstairs in the kitchen. And the short time my parents, who definitely loved each other, had together. And my grandmother, who has spent so much of her life living alone. And Natalie's parents, who are friends but are apart.

"It would be amazing." I pause, and then I ask, "Is this like our epilogue?"

"Danny," Natalie says without hesitation. "I think this is the beginning of a beautiful friendship."

I know that's a line from a famous movie. I don't know which one. But it doesn't matter. Because this isn't a movie. There is no script. There is no map.

If it is possible, we will find our way together.

Acknowledgements

I have never constructed a cardboard unicorn. I've not been chased by television cameras. Except for the time I accidentally knocked Sally Fields onto the ground and then fell on top of her, I haven't spent significant time with Hollywood celebrities. And yet, there is very little in Danny Constantino's story that feels made up to me. That's because I am surrounded by family, friends, makers, and mentors who believe that fun, failure, adventures, and joy are almost always worth sharing. So if I know you and you found a story or scene in this book that sounds kind of familiar... thank you!

Of course, as it says on the copyright page, this is a work of fiction, and any resemblance to actual persons, living or dead, is entirely coincidental.

Wink. Wink.

Here are a few incontrovertible facts: This book would not exist without great enthusiasm, faith, and guidance from my editor Nancy Mercado and my agent, Susan Hawk. They are extraordinary book-making partners and trusted friends as well as all-around awesome human beings. I am very grateful to Neil Swaab for illustrating the cover, and to the entire Penguin team including Rosie Ahmed, Regina Castillo, Maria Fazio, Theresa Evangelista, Cerise Steel and many more whose work behind the scenes brings books to life. Also, I owe special thanks to my publisher Lauri Hornik for welcoming me home to Dial Books for Young Readers!

Finally, I cannot imagine writing a book about family, friendship, laughter, and romance if those things were not very real in my own life. It would be impossible to list every person who has ever given those gifts to me. It is equally impossible to describe how thankful I am to be married to the love of my life who is also my very best friend. I love you, Debbie.